A BRIDE FOR DONNIGAN

Books by Janette Oke

www.janetteoke.com

Another Homecoming* / Tomorrow's Dream*
Dana's Valley† • Nana's Gift
The Red Geranium • Return to Harmony*

CANADIAN WEST

When Calls the Heart   When Breaks the Dawn
When Comes the Spring   When Hope Springs New

Beyond the Gathering Storm
When Tomorrow Comes

LOVE COMES SOFTLY

Love Comes Softly   Love's Unending Legacy
Love's Enduring Promise   Love's Unfolding Dream
Love's Long Journey   Love Takes Wing
Love's Abiding Joy   Love Finds a Home

A PRAIRIE LEGACY

The Tender Years   A Quiet Strength
A Searching Heart   Like Gold Refined

SEASONS OF THE HEART

Once Upon a Summer   Winter Is Not Forever
The Winds of Autumn   Spring's Gentle Promise

SONG OF ACADIA*

The Meeting Place   The Birthright
The Sacred Shore   The Distant Beacon
The Beloved Land

WOMEN OF THE WEST

The Calling of Emily Evans   A Bride for Donnigan
Julia's Last Hope   Heart of the Wilderness
Roses for Mama   Too Long a Stranger
A Woman Named Damaris   The Bluebird and the Sparrow
They Called Her Mrs. Doc   A Gown of Spanish Lace
The Measure of a Heart   Drums of Change

––––––––

Janette Oke: A Heart for the Prairie
Biography of Janette Oke by Laurel Oke Logan

*with T. Davis Bunn   †with Laurel Oke Logan

JANETTE OKE

A BRIDE FOR DONNIGAN

BETHANY HOUSE PUBLISHERS
MINNEAPOLIS, MINNESOTA 55438

Published by Bethany House Publishers
A Ministry of Bethany Fellowship International
11400 Hampshire Avenue South
Minneapolis, Minnesota 55438
www.bethanyhouse.com

Printed in the United States of America by
Bethany Press International, Minneapolis, Minnesota 55438

Library of Congress Cataloging-in-Publication Data

Oke, Janette, 1935–
   A bride for Donnigan / Janette Oke.
     p. cm.

   1. Women pioneers—Fiction. I. Title.
PR9199.3.O38B73   1993
813'.54—dc20   92–46297
ISBN 1–55661–327–X   CIP
ISBN 1–55661–328–8 (Large Print)

To the special cousins
I grew up with—
Bob, Don, Richard, Tom, Kenneth Archie
And Eva

JANETTE OKE was born in Champion, Alberta, during the depression years, to a Canadian prairie farmer and his wife. She is a graduate of Mountain View Bible College in Didsbury, Alberta, where she met her husband, Edward. They were married in May of 1957, and went on to pastor churches in Indiana as well as Calgary and Edmonton, Canada.

The Okes have three sons and one daughter and are enjoying the addition to the family of grandchildren. Edward and Janette have both been active in their local church, serving in various capacities as Sunday-school teachers and board members. They make their home in Didsbury, Alberta.

Contents

Prologue

This series of WOMEN OF THE WEST has presented a number of different personalities in various circumstances that women of the past faced, and it seems right that a little attention be given to those who came, "sight unseen," to the Americas to be brides of frontier men.

We know from history that these marriages did occur. But what do we really know about them? What would move a man to seek a complete stranger to be his lifelong mate? What kind of woman would respond to such a request? How might she feel as she traveled over oceans and frontiers to get to her unknown destination? Did the marriages indeed *work*?

I don't pretend to have all the answers—but from a little research and with a little imagination, we can journey with one such couple to that significant first meeting and experience some of the emotions they must have felt on the way to that moment—and afterward.

Chapter One

Kathleen

She stood for a long time staring through the dark of the morning mist at the posted notice. Her lips moved ever so slightly as she read again the strange words by the aid of the flickering streetlamp beside them—then read them once more to make sure she understood their meaning.

"Ladies!" The word seemed to shout off the printed paper. "The Opportunity of a Lifetime in the New American Frontier! Well-Secured Ranchers, Farmers, and Businessmen Desire Wedded Partners to Share Their Life and Prosperity. INQUIRE WITHIN."

"Surely it doesn't mean . . ." She mentally began an argument with the words. But she didn't even finish the unspoken statement. Her eyes were locked on the notice, and she read it through for the fourth time.

"Would a girl—a woman really think of. . . ?" Her argument picked up again. "No, surely not. I never could even—even *think* of such a thing."

But a few of the phrases still clung to her mind. "Well-secured." "Prosperity." And then the strange little phrase "wedded partners." Did it really mean what she thought it did? She could only imagine one possibility. But she had never heard the phrase "wedded partners" before. Was the sign really saying that men—somewhere—were *advertising for wives*?

Her slight shoulders gave just a hint of a shrug. The thin

coat, much too small even for her tiny frame, was reluctant to allow even that much room. She seemed to shrink back within its strained seams. The chill of the early morning made her shiver slightly in spite of her resolve to endure the cold.

"Sure now, and I'd best be on or I'll be late for my hawking," she scolded herself and was about to leave when two other young women approached quickly—excitedly.

"There—ya see it for your own eyes. I wasn't yarnin'. Look—right there."

Kathleen did not have time to move away from the notice on the wall. The girls seemed not to see her, so intent were they on their mission. They shoved right past her, and the taller of the two read the notice aloud for the shorter, more sturdy one. Kathleen took a step backward and hoped she was hidden in the shadows.

"Ladies. The opportunity of a lifetime in the new American frontier. Well-secured ranchers, farmers, and businessmen desire wedded partners to share their life and prosperity. Inquire within." There could be no mistake—the now-familiar words had been confirmed by another.

"Well, I never—!" exclaimed the shorter girl, and the two clutched each other and hooted and squealed. Kathleen found her cheeks staining red. For a reason she couldn't quite understand, she felt embarrassed.

"And you're thinking to apply?" demanded the shorter girl.

"Aye, Erma," answered the taller, a bit of Scottish brogue tinting her words. "And I've already done."

"No! Go on with ya, lass!"

Another squeal. Another shriek of laughter.

"And why not? There's no *prosperity* to be had here in London. Not for the likes of me."

"But to leave home—"

"*Home?* Home has been little more than the streets for me—"

She broke off, but her words trembled in the cold, early morning air. Both girls became instantly serious, and Kathleen again shivered in her thin coat.

"Do you think—? I mean, do you really think that a body—well, might. . . ?" The one called Erma was unable to finish the sentence.

"What's to lose?" said her companion with an obvious shrug of her broad shoulders. "We have nothing here."

Erma nodded. "And you've already signed up? What do you have to do? I mean, do you need to have a dowry? Make promises?"

"Just give your name and promise to be there on the day of sailin', that's all."

"It can't be that easy."

"But it is, I tell you. They're already holdin' a passage ticket with my name on it. I saw it for myself."

Kathleen stirred in the shadows. She had to get to work. She would lose her job if she didn't; and though it wasn't much, it was all she had, and it did bring in a few pence each week.

It was the first time the two girls seemed to notice her. Their heads jerked around in quick attention, but when they saw the slight girl move into the light they visibly relaxed.

"You gave me a start, dearie," said the bigger, taller girl.

"Sure, and I'm sorry," apologized Kathleen, her Irish accent becoming thicker with her discomfort.

"No need to fret," said the shorter Erma. "No harm done." Her voice was soft and friendly, and Kathleen felt herself drawn to her immediately. She wished—but she quickly chided herself and shook her shoulders as though to also shake off her desire for the unattainable. Yet it would be so nice—so nice to have a real friend.

"Are you thinkin' of signing up?" Erma continued, her eyes still on Kathleen.

Kathleen was about to make quick denial but Erma went on.

"Peg here has already signed. Says there's nothing to it. I . . ." The girl hesitated, then lifted her chin as though suddenly coming to her own resolve. "I'm thinkin' on signing myself."

The bigger girl, Peg, gave a squeal and reached to impetuously give her friend a hug.

"I need to get to my work," apologized Kathleen, moving to leave. "I'll be losing me job and that's the truth."

Peg cut in quickly. "When we get to America, we won't need to worry none about hawkin' posies in the street or sweepin' out the city gutters." Then she stopped and seemed to look more closely at the slender girl before her. "You've a pretty face," she observed candidly. "They'd be right glad to have you sign."

Kathleen stopped mid-stride. She opened her mouth but no words came out. She felt her face flushing again.

"If you're thinkin' on signin'," the girl named Peg said in a confidential tone, "don't wait too long. They only have room on ship for about twenty, and the passages are being taken real fast."

"Where do you sign?" Erma asked Peg quickly.

"Right there—through that door. I'll take ya in," said Peg excitedly. The two girls turned toward the door and Kathleen stood and watched them go, feeling alone and forgotten.

"If you decide to join us, we'd be most happy to travel with ya," Erma flung back over her shoulder.

So she had not been forgotten, after all.

Kathleen stirred herself once more. She had to get to work. She pulled her thin coat more closely about her shoulders, took a deep breath and moved forward. She needed to make up for lost time. If only she could hurry. If only— She shook the thoughts from her head and hunched into the biting morning air. She couldn't hurry and that was that. She would do the best she could to make up for lost work time. And she started off down the dark, dirty streets, her body rocking slightly with each step she took. The decided limp had been with her for as long as she could remember.

The day did not go well. Kathleen had been a few minutes late in spite of her extra effort to get there on time. The old man who ran the bakery had been terribly upset with her. He scolded and swore and threatened to cut her pay. She knew and he knew that if he did, she'd never hear the end of it from Madam.

Madam! Kathleen inwardly hated the title, though she had never allowed herself the pleasure of hating the person. She was, after all, the only mum she had. She was, after all, the woman whom her father had married two years after the death of her own mother. Kathleen, who had been a child of three when her mother died, had few memories of her own mother, but what she had she cherished.

Madam was the woman who had taken over the home and the man who was Kathleen's father. The woman who had presented him with a daughter and two sons. Three children that Kathleen herself had tended more than their mother had. Three children who were more than a little spoiled and difficult. But regardless of their faults, three children that Kathleen had quickly learned to love.

The years had not been kind to Kathleen. At seven she had lost the grandmother who had tried in her own limited way to shield and protect her. Also at a very early age she was expected to take on a mammoth portion of the household duties in spite of her thin frame and the limp that had been there since she learned to walk.

"She needs to learn the care of a house," defended the woman who insisted that Kathleen address her as Madam because of her French heritage.

Kathleen's father had nodded slowly. He did not interfere with "matters of the household," but Kathleen thought she read concern in his eyes many times.

So Kathleen had learned to do all the housekeeping chores by the time she was ten. She had also been nursemaid to the little ones, which included getting up in the night, changing their nappies, and taking them to Madam for the nighttime feedings. The limp that had begun as slight became more and more pronounced as she carted heavy babies and full laundry baskets on her tiny hip.

"She'll never marry," Madam complained to Kathleen's

father, fretting about the limp.

"Nonsense." Kathleen was surprised to hear him dare to argue. "Look at her pretty face."

"But a pretty face won't be enough. It might turn heads—but they'll quickly turn away when they see her take a step."

"I won't hear such drivel," Kathleen was surprised to hear her father state, his voice firm with command. Apparently he *did* still feel he was master in his own home. "Kathleen is intelligent and pretty. One is not—not brushed aside and discredited for—for one small flaw. Such—such drivel. Sure now—I will hear nothing of it again."

As far as Kathleen knew, Madam never spoke to her father about the limp again, but she did speak to the girl. Over and over, when the two were alone and Kathleen hurried as best she could about the house scrubbing laundry, preparing supper, or tending babies, the woman clicked and pratted over the girl's "unfortunate condition." Kathleen burned with the humiliation and unfairness of it.

And then had come the most difficult event of her young life. Her father became sick and, in just two months' time, had been taken from them. Madam ranted and raved. The man had left her, alone, with five mouths to feed. Kathleen was no longer asked to stay at home and care for the household—though most of those same tasks were still awaiting her when she returned home at nights, tired from a long day in the streets. It was not easy to find the job that Madam sent her off to secure. She was thirteen and frail and basically unskilled except in household chores. She could read and do sums—her father had seen to that.

As Madam had warned again and again, her limp figured into her success in finding employment. Most shopkeepers did not want her as an apprentice. They feared the customers would be unnerved as she moved about to serve them. Nor was she to be accepted as a governess. Only the old man at the bakery had seen her limp as a possible asset. People, bless their souls, often responded to a handicap. With her small, sensitive, and pretty face, combined with the pathetic limp that wasn't even a carefully practiced put-on, Kathleen might prove to be a good source of income selling his penny rolls and tuppence meat pies.

He had been right. Kathleen sold more wares than any of his other hawkers—though he had never revealed that fact to her. Daily he lived in fear that Kathleen might find a job elsewhere or meet some young man who would wish to make her his wife. So when she arrived a few minutes late after stopping to read the posting, the man was beside himself with worry. What if he lost her? A good share of his daily profits would be lost as well.

When she did appear, he scolded and raged and piled her basket with a larger than usual load of his baked goods.

"And mind ya get right on with it," he fumed. "Ye've already lost half the mornin' crowd."

Kathleen struggled under the weight of the load. Silently she went back out into the cold to peddle the breads and pastries.

As she called out to passersby and collected the pennies for the sale, her mind went back again and again to the words in the notice. "Well-secured. Prosperous. Wedded partners." Would a man from the American frontier be willing to accept a wife with a limp? No, it was unthinkable. But the words still stayed in her mind to haunt her throughout the entire day. She wished—she *almost* wished—that she were one of the other girls. Like Peg, tall and straight with broad shoulders and a strong back. Or the shorter one named Erma. She had such kind eyes. Such a soft voice. The girl was plump and solid, not scrawny and slight. She would have no trouble pleasing a frontier husband, with her robustness and friendly demeanor.

Then Peg's words returned to her thinking. "You have a pretty face. They'd be right glad to have you sign up."

But Peg had not known of her limp.

Just as quickly, the words of Madam came to mind. "But a pretty face won't be enough. They'll turn away when they see her take the first step."

It was true—even a frontier man would never accept the likes of her as a "wedded partner."

_____

At the end of the long, difficult day, Kathleen made her way home through the gray streets, the gray buildings now enshrouded with gray fog. The gray gutters were almost hidden by the deeper gray shadows. Her shoulders drooped with weariness. Her steps dragged, accenting her limp.

Undoubtedly the week's washing was still to be rubbed out on the scrubboard. There was supper to prepare. She did hope that young Bridget had been sent to the shops for meat and vegetables. When the days were damp and chill with fog, the younger girl often refused to go.

Kathleen loved Bridget in spite of her willfulness. There was no way that she could have withheld her love. The girl looked like their father. Kathleen, he had told her over and over before his untimely death, was the picture of her mother. So Kathleen mothered Bridget, even as Madam spoiled her. Kathleen did so want the young girl to grow up to be a credit to their father. To that end, she pleaded and scolded and fussed at her young half sister, teaching her manners, letters, and sums. For the most part the girls got along well—unless Madam interfered and chided Kathleen for "demanding" too much of one "so young and delicate."

Kathleen reached the small cottage and pushed open the heavy iron gate with her shoulder. The gate growled and whined on its rusty hinges.

"And if Father were here, he would use some oil," Kathleen said to herself. "It won't be long until it'll refuse to budge."

A deep sigh escaped her as she moved toward the crumbling concrete step. She dreaded to enter the room and deposit her few small coins on the kitchen table. The house, always dark with gloom since her father had died, represented so much work to be done. She wished that she could just— What? She didn't really know. All she knew was that she wished she didn't have to lift the latch and cross the threshold into the dank kitchen chamber, the gloom, and Madam. But enter she must.

She put her hand on the door latch and dragged her reluctant foot up to the last step.

With a flurry that was totally unexpected, the door jerked inward out of her grasp. There stood Bridget, hair tossed, cheeks flushed, hands clapping to her breast. "Kathleen!" she shrieked. "You'll never guess what has just happened! Mama is marrying again!"

Chapter Two

Donnigan

"Whoa."

The man shifted slightly to draw back on the reins he held firmly in a large, calloused hand. The big black he was riding immediately responded to the command, though he tossed his head and champed on the bit. The man smiled and reached out his other hand to stroke the wind-swept mane. The horse's neck was warm and damp with sweat beneath his touch. They had both enjoyed the run.

He swung one long leg over the horse's back and stepped down from the saddle. As he moved away, the horse followed, still working on the bit and tossing his head.

"Don't be so impatient," the man said, but the tone was gentle and his voice was low and deep, touched softly with the drawl of the south.

His eyes swept the fields before him. It was his first crop— and the grain he had planted already stood tall on sturdy stocks. He couldn't hide the sparkle in his eyes, but the big stallion who rubbed his nose impatiently on his master's shirt sleeve did not seem to notice.

"Look at it, Black," he said to the horse, for he had to speak to someone. "Best crop I've ever seen."

The black just snorted.

He stood for several more minutes surveying his fields, then turned back to the horse. "Don't know why you're always in such a hurry," he scolded. "We've got all day."

But the black blew and lifted his head. As he felt the reins being gathered once again, he tossed his head at this signal that they were about to resume their journey.

The horse was big, but the man was in direct proportion. He was tall, being six foot two, his shoulders broad, his arms tight with muscles built by hard work on the land. Thick blond hair above a ruddy complexion and a pleasant expression completed the picture.

He swung up into the saddle easily and lifted the reins. The black jerked around eagerly and sprang to a gallop back across the ridge the moment he felt the touch of heel to his side.

When they reached the fork in the trail, the man turned the horse eastward instead of toward the building site, and the stallion did not hesitate. He knew every trail of the farm almost as well as his master, and this direction took them to the pastures where cattle and horses fed lazily on plentiful prairie grass.

They had to stop to open a gate. The horse stomped and snorted his impatience, but the man was slow and deliberate in each movement. "Easy, Black. Easy," he drawled softly as the large animal tugged on the reins.

They entered the pastures together, and the man turned back to lift into position the wooden post that supported the gate wires, slipping the loop of wire over the top to fasten it securely. Then he remounted and they were off again.

By now the sides of the black were shiny with sweat, but the man still had to hold the horse in check.

The man's closest neighbor, Wallis Tremont, had once observed, "I think thet horse'd run 'til he dropped." His voice had conveyed his admiration as he looked at the animal.

Donnigan smiled now at the thought and had to admit that Wallis likely was right. The black sure did love to run.

Man and horse crossed a small creek, wound their way up a hill, and topped the crest to look out over a sweeping valley. There beneath them grazed fifty-odd head of prime stock. The sparkle returned to Donnigan's eyes, and a slow smile turned up the corners of his mouth and crinkled the tanned skin around his eyes.

"Spring calves sure do look good," he told the horse.

The black pawed the ground.

"I know, I know," he said with a chuckle. "You want to see the horses."

But he did not give the horse permission to move on. Not just yet. He loved to look out at the herd as it grazed peacefully in the valley. He had long dreamed of just such a scene before him. His. Yet even now he could scarcely believe that the dream had actually come true.

Oh, not all of it. He still had a ways to go. Still had fences to build and buildings to raise. And there were the payments to make. His crops were still in the fields. His herds were not the size he hoped to make them. But the crops looked good. The herds would take care of their own growth. He had good stock. That was what counted. And time would take care of the line of annual payments that stretched out before him. He felt good. Blessed. Happy. He was right where he wanted to be—and still young enough to enjoy many years of being there.

Donnigan's body shifted as the big black beneath him pawed the ground again and snorted his annoyance at being kept in check.

"All right. All right," said the man, for the first time just a hint of impatience in his voice.

He lifted the reins and urged the horse forward. "So where do you think they'll be feeding?"

The black did not wait for a second invitation. With a toss of his head he headed south, taking the rise in long, powerful strides, the foam on his broad chest flecking the man who sat in the saddle.

"Easy. Easy," Donnigan chided gently, his hand slightly tightening the reins.

They topped the rise, and there they were—three geldings, seven mares, and six foals. At the sound of the approaching hooves all heads lifted and excited whinnies welcomed the black. One mare left the herd and trotted toward them, her head held high, her nostrils distended. Other mares joined her, trotting a few paces, stopping, snorting, tossing heads and swishing tails. The geldings shifted about, seeming uneasy at the appearance of the black stallion. Only the younger foals seemed unaffected. They fed or gambolled or chased after dams just as though the big black was not quickly covering the distance between them.

Donnigan rode right up to the shifting herd. They swirled and bolted around him, and though his demeanor seemed just as relaxed, his eyes were ever alert for the playful kick that could mean a bad bruise or even a broken leg should it strike a rider.

"Look at that young colt," he said to his black. "You ought to be plenty proud of him. He looks just like you."

The colt was playfully nipping another foal and dancing and kicking in mock battle.

The black paid no more attention to the colt than to the rest of the milling herd.

Donnigan studied each of his horses carefully. For the most part he was more than pleased with what he saw, but his eyes did narrow when he saw Sergeant, one of his work geldings, appear to move forward with a very slight limp. He seemed to be favoring his right front leg. Donnigan watched the horse take a few more steps, his eyes squinted against the harsh afternoon sun, and then he lifted his rope from the saddle horn and moved the black into closer proximity.

With one quick flick of his wrist the rope snaked out and encircled the neck of the surprised roan. He did not fight the noose about his neck, but his head lifted and he snorted his complaint.

Donnigan moved the black to a hold position and swung down from the saddle.

"Whoa, boy. Whoa, Sarg," he soothed as he moved along the rope to the gelding.

Gently his hands began to rub the nose, caress the neck, and then slide down toward the right front foot. The horse responded by lifting the foot when the hand reached the hoof. Donnigan was relieved at what he found. No serious problem, simply a small stone lodged against the frog.

Holding the hoof with one hand against his bent knee,

he reached into his pants pocket and withdrew his knife.
After opening the blade with his teeth, he began to gently
nudge the stone from its wedged position, all the while talking soothingly to the horse.

When the stone was gone, Donnigan ran a practiced finger over the entire area. There seemed to be no damage—no
swelling. The horse should be fine.

Patting the gelding again, he released the leg and slipped
the noose from the roan's neck. The horse did not step back
but reached instead to rub his nose against the tall man's
shoulder.

"Go on with you. Get outta here," said Donnigan affectionately with another slap on the animal's neck. "You won't
be needed in the hay field for a few days yet."

The roan flung his head and moved slowly away, and Donnigan made his way back to the black, coiling his rope as he
moved.

He replaced the rope on the saddle horn and reached for
the reins. His eyes passed over the herd that had gradually
stopped its shifting and returned to grazing.

"See that, Black. They're ignoring you already," Donnigan chuckled and rubbed the horse's nose. Then his eyes
lifted to the sky. It was a clear, sunny day. A perfect day for—
something. But Donnigan wasn't sure just what he would do
with it.

It would be another week before the hay was ready. The
crops were well on the way but far from harvest. The fences
were mended, the barn cleaned and strawed. With plenty of
water and feed, the cattle needed no care in the summer
months. The horses had just been checked. The roan was now
moving about with little trace of his former limp.

"Guess we aren't needed here," he said to the stallion.
"Might as well head on home."

He gathered up the reins and stepped up into the saddle
again. The black shifted and snorted. Donnigan knew that
the horse would prefer staying with the herd. But it was
almost two miles back to the house, and Donnigan had never
enjoyed walking for no good reason. And he certainly had no

intention of walking that afternoon in the hot sun with a saddle on his shoulder.

"Come on," he urged the black as he laid the rein against his neck to swing him around. "You'll be with the herd soon enough."

Then he added softly as though to himself, "At least you got a herd to go to. Me? I have to content myself with having conversations with critters."

And suddenly the joy seemed gone from the day. It was wonderful to have a dream fulfilled—but he sure was lonely.

———

By the time Donnigan had reached the farm buildings, the cloud of discontent had settled firmly about him. Not one to be given to brooding, he tried hard to shake the feeling. Surely, he reasoned, when he reached home and looked at the snug frame cabin that was his, the sturdy log buildings that were his barn and outbuildings, the strong, upright fences and corrals that he had spent days laboring over, the mood would leave him.

But even as he reined Black in before the corral gate and prepared to dismount, he realized he still felt discomfited.

He wanted to shake himself. To rid himself of his morose thoughts. To chide himself for feeling "down" when he had just surveyed so much that should make him feel "up."

"What's gone wrong?" he said aloud and realized that he was not talking to the black but to himself.

He had no answer. He just felt—yes, lonely. But surely a man who lived alone had a right to his lonely times. It seemed natural enough.

But as Donnigan moved to give the stallion his rubdown and return him to the corral, to the trough filled with clear spring water and to the manger filled with sweet hay, his thoughts were not easy to shake.

He was even more troubled when the black moved away from the water and hay and straight to the corral fence that was the closest he could get to the distant herd. He pushed his large body against the rails and lifted his head in a long, plaintive whinny.

The lonely call of the stallion seemed to shake Donnigan to his very soul. For a moment he regretted that he hadn't left the horse in the pasture with the herd and walked home through the heat. It seemed cruel to separate him from his kind.

In the next moment Donnigan lifted the saddle from the rail where he had placed it, then whistled to the horse. The black swung around, tossing his head and trotting obediently toward Donnigan.

"Don't get too excited," Donnigan warned him gently. "We're not going back to the herd. But I gotta talk with someone before I go stir crazy. We're gonna go see Wallis."

———

As expected, the stallion had wanted to take the trail back toward the pasture, but with a gentle nudge on the rein, Donnigan urged him toward the rough tract that was the country road. Black didn't argue, being too well trained to fight the command. Soon they were loping easily in the direction of the neighbor bachelor's place.

Donnigan wondered if they would find Wallis at home, but as they swung down the lane, Donnigan saw the man come to his door and peer out into the bright sun. Then the door swung fully open and Wallis squinted out at them.

"Tie yer horse and come in," he invited. "I was just gettin' myself some grub."

It seemed too late for dinner and too early for supper in Donnigan's thinking, but he only smiled. Wallis was not known to keep another man's time schedule.

He tied Black and followed the man into his shack, beating the road dust from his chaps with his Stetson as he walked.

The one room of the small cabin was in its usual disarray.

"Pull up a chair," invited Wallis.

Donnigan picked up a broken bridle and tossed it on the

floor in the corner as he took the chair Wallis indicated.

"I've had my dinner," Donnigan informed him as he moved toward the stove. "Just a cup of coffee."

Wallis lifted a coffee cup from the bit of cupboard and swished a dirty piece of dish towel around its interior. Then he reached for the heavy enamel pot and poured a cup of the black, steamy liquid. Without comment Donnigan accepted the cup and took a sip. It was strong as tar and as hot as shoeing tongs. He put it down on the table and licked his lips to cool them.

"So what brings you out?" said Wallis around a bite of bread and gravy. "You're usually too busy fer neighboring in broad daylight."

Donnigan smiled. "In between chores," he said without rancor. "Hay's not quite ready yet. Thought I might just get a little visit in."

Donnigan dared another guarded sip of coffee, looking at Wallis over the cup's rim. His eyes had taken on a certain knowing glint.

"Went to town the other day," Wallis said slowly, as though wanting to check his tongue but unable to keep his news to himself. "Got myself a paper."

Donnigan didn't see anything too extraordinary about that.

"Had me a talk with Lucas, too."

Donnigan knew Lucas well. He was the man who ran the local livery, stagecoach, and hotel. He had done right well for himself, folks said. In fact, he might be one who would become rich in the new West.

Donnigan sipped the coffee and nodded, waiting for Wallis to go on with his story about Lucas—or the paper—whatever it was that was making Wallis's eyes take on the shine.

But Wallis jumped right into the matter, his expression bright.

"Did ya know thet a man can order hisself a wife?" asked Wallis.

Donnigan suddenly swallowed more coffee than he had

intended. He sucked in air quickly to try to cool his scalded throat.

"Can what?" he exclaimed in disbelief.

"Can order a bride," declared Wallis.

Donnigan replaced the cup to the table slowly, frowning as he tried to comprehend the statement. "Go on!" he said at length. "You're funnin'."

"Ain't neither," declared Wallis, sounding just a bit put out. "Saw it with my own eyes. Right there in black and white."

Donnigan knew that Wallis could read nothing more than his name. He bought papers for show. A slow smile began to touch his lips. If Wallis wasn't joking, someone else was having fun at his expense.

"Who showed you?" he asked cautiously. He didn't want to offend Wallis, but he was sure now that someone had played a mean trick on the man.

"Lucas. Lucas hisself. He's sending fer one. Got her all signed up. They're bringing in a whole shipment of 'em. Be here by fall."

Donnigan could not believe his ears. The whole idea was preposterous. No. No, it was worse than that. It was degrading. Inhuman. What man would ever order a wife the same way he would buy an animal for his herd? A kettle for his kitchen? It was totally unacceptable. Unthinkable. Totally.

"I'm gettin' my money rounded up now. Almost got enough fer the ticket. You've been sayin' thet you'd like a few hogs—well, I got a couple I'll sell. Two young sows ready to farrow."

He stopped for a breath and Donnigan stared at him, still in disbelief.

"Well? Ya interested or not? If ya ain't, I'll load 'em up and take 'em into town. Someone'll want 'em."

This joke has gone too far, Donnigan was thinking. *The man is serious about this and—*

"Well?" prompted Wallis again, and Donnigan pulled his attention back to the query.

"Sure. Sure," he responded slowly. "I'm interested. I'll take 'em—the hogs, that is."

"Good," said Wallis, and Donnigan saw the light in the man's eyes again. Wallis rubbed his palms together as though he could not wait.

Donnigan felt sick. What could he say? At least until he had talked with the errant Lucas. But even the thought of Lucas made him shift uneasily. Lucas was not a man for joking around. If it had been Sam Cook or Pete Rawlings who had sold Wallis the bizarre story, Donnigan might have expected such nonsense. But Lucas!

Suddenly Donnigan knew he had to get to the bottom of the tale. He had to save Wallis from total embarrassment. He rose from his chair.

"I'd best be going," he said.

Wallis looked up from his gravied bread.

"What's yer hurry? Ya just got here."

"I—I need to ride on into town," Donnigan said lamely. Then quickly added, "When ya needin' the money?"

"By Friday," responded Wallis. "I want a wife from thet next shipment. They don't bring in another 'til spring, and I don't want to go through another long winter talkin' to myself."

Donnigan felt the loneliness of the man pierce his own soul. He understood about talking to oneself. He hadn't realized Wallis had felt that way, too.

"By Friday," he repeated, his mouth suddenly dry. "I'll have it for you by then."

He turned to go, noticing as he did that his coffee cup still held some of the black substance. Would Wallis be offended? Donnigan lifted the cup and drained it with one gulp. It was no longer scalding hot but was still just as bitter. He nodded at Wallis and reached for his Stetson.

He was about to duck his way out the creaking door when Wallis stopped him in his tracks. "Ya gonna sign up for one?" Wallis quizzed, the excitement in his voice again.

Donnigan did not even answer the question. He felt sick inside.

Chapter Three

Decided

Kathleen could not have been more shocked. She was aware that Madam had a social life outside the home. Madam kept company with a Mrs. Mercer, who introduced her to woman friends, and supposedly gentlemen as well, but Kathleen had never stopped to think of the possibility of another marriage. She stood now with her mouth open at the announcement from Bridget.

"Well, don't stand there letting in all the damp and cold," Madam scolded, entering the small room from the living area.

Kathleen moved forward and closed the door. Her eyes studied the face of the woman and she saw a flush in her cheeks. She longed to ask if Bridget had spoken the truth, but her tongue didn't seem to work.

"Why do you stand at the door when there is so much to be done? The supper isn't even—"

"I just told her about your coming marriage," interrupted Bridget.

The older woman stopped and flushed deeper, her eyes beginning to glow by the lamplight. Her hand fluttered nervously to tuck a stray wisp of hair under her day bonnet. But she gave no other response.

"I—I—" Kathleen did not know what to say. What was she expected to say? "I had no idea," she finally managed lamely.

"You are never here to inform," snipped the woman. "Mr. Withers does his calling by day, and you are always gone."

Kathleen was well aware of how her days were spent.

"He's a jolly fine old boy," cut in Edmund, Kathleen's eight-year-old half brother, as he held out the candy stick that the gentleman had obviously brought him.

"Watch your tongue," countered Madam. "You will show more respect."

The boy quickly sidestepped the hand that would have cuffed his ear. His eyes danced merrily as he laughed at his mother's failed, weak effort toward correction, and he left the room, still licking his candy treat.

"He *is* pleasant," Bridget assured her older half sister. "He has even promised that I may go away to the Academy."

The thought of Bridget leaving brought an unexpected stab to Kathleen's heart.

"Charles is to go off to school, too," went on Bridget.

"Oh, dear!" exclaimed Kathleen. It seemed that there had been a whole host of changes in her life in a few brief hours.

"And we will even be moving," broke in Charles, who had just entered the room. "To the countryside. I can hardly wait. I do hope I can have my own pony."

"Moving?" Kathleen cast a quick glance in the direction of her stepmother.

The woman just nodded as she began smoothing the lapel of Charles's jacket. She was always fussing over Charles. Kathleen had long observed that he was his mother's pet.

"Moving where?" Kathleen dared to ask.

"Now you needn't bother your head none about it," said the woman, as though all the changes would not affect Kathleen in the least. "Right now we are in need of our supper. We will have plenty of time to discuss the future after we have eaten. Put it on to cook, and while you are waiting you can start the scrubbing. I'll need my blue dress for tomorrow. It needs freshening. Mind you watch that the color does not run into the white collar."

With those words she turned and left the room, shooing her offspring ahead of her.

Bridget looked back over her shoulder. "I put the meat in the back cupboard," she called. Kathleen was relieved that the supper items had been purchased.

At the same time, she felt the anger within her burning her cheeks. Why was she always treated like a—like a common domestic? Quickly Kathleen pushed the anger aside. She should be thankful that she had a family, a home—just as Madam was always reminding her. Daily she saw girls her age who lived totally on the streets. Their lot was not a good one.

Suddenly her thin coat seemed heavy on her shoulders. She shrugged out of it and hung it on the peg by the back door. Marriage! She had never thought of the possibility. Though she didn't know why it had not occurred to her. Madam was still a young woman. And she was still appealing—in her own sort of way. Kathleen really should not be surprised to hear that a gentleman friend had proposed marriage to her stepmother.

Tired and chilled to the bone, she moved to the cupboard and began to prepare the supper vegetables and meat. She wished there was not laundry to do. It had been such a long and difficult day.

Then a thought came that lifted her spirits somewhat. With the marriage—and the move to the country—she would no longer need to tramp the dull back streets of London each day, calling out her wares. For that much she could be thankful.

She added coal to the kitchen stove. With the warmth of the fire cooking the evening meal and bending over heated scrub water, she was sure to feel warm again before long. She almost welcomed the thought of plunging her hands into the hot suds. She hastened to get the meat on to cook.

"I know that Mama said you didn't know Mr. Withers because you are never home when he calls," said Bridget after they had retired that night.

Kathleen nodded silently into the darkness.

"But do you know what I think?" went on the younger girl. "I think Mama doesn't want you to know him."

Kathleen stirred restlessly.

"Or—that Mama didn't want *him* to know you—I'm not sure which," went on the young girl candidly.

"What do you mean?" asked Kathleen.

"Well, either Mama was afraid that he'd think you pretty or—"

Kathleen couldn't believe the girl's ridiculous statement, but young Bridget hurried on. "Mama has always been jealous of you, you know. Papa often said that you looked like—like your mama, and—well, my mama didn't like it. She feared he preferred—"

"That's ridiculous!" Kathleen cut in quickly.

"You might say so—but it's true," Bridget insisted. And then she added, quite unknowing of how deeply her words hurt her older sister, "But of course she is also ashamed of your limp. She has always been afraid that someone will think you are her child, and she doesn't want a—a—cripple. She seems to fear that a man will think there is something wrong with *her*. That she might—might mother another child in—in even worse condition. I think that's the real reason she made sure that Mr. Withers has never had the opportunity to meet you. She keeps saying to him—oh, I've heard her myself, 'There are four of us. I have three children.' And she presents us just as though that's all there are."

There was silence.

"Kathleen? Have you fallen asleep while I'm talking?" Bridget asked into the darkness.

"No," came the soft reply.

"Why don't you answer?" prompted her half sister.

"What should I say?" responded Kathleen. Indeed, it seemed that the plans for the future had been made with no thought given to her.

"When we move—" began Bridget, but Kathleen interrupted.

"When *you* move," she corrected. "Sure now, can't you see,

Bridget? There are no plans for me to move with you."

Bridget stirred beside her in the darkness. Kathleen heard the sharp intake of breath and was sure the younger girl had not fully understood the situation before.

"I won't go without you," Bridget declared, her hand reaching out to grasp the arm of Kathleen's nightgown. "I won't." Her voice rose sharply, and Kathleen feared that her outburst would awaken the woman who slept just beyond the thin wall.

"Sh-h-h," she cautioned.

"Well, I won't."

"Sh-h-h," Kathleen said again, and her own hand went out to rest on the younger girl's flanneled shoulder.

"What will you do?" Bridget finally asked, a sob in her voice.

"I have my job," said Kathleen with more assurance than she felt.

"But where would you live?"

It was a question Kathleen could not answer, but she tried to keep her voice controlled as she responded with seemingly little concern. "There are places. Lots of places." But even as she said the words, she knew she could afford none of them on a hawker's pennies.

"When is the wedding—?" she began.

"Mama's? The end of the month. We will stay here until then. I heard Mr. Withers and Mama making their plans. He will send a carriage for our things and on the day of the wedding—"

But Kathleen wished to hear no more.

"We must get some sleep," she told the younger girl. "I was late for work this morning—and I don't want to be late again. I will need to be up early to get breakfast on."

The younger girl did not respond. Kathleen patted her arm in the darkness to let her know that she was not upset with her, then rolled over onto her side to try to get some much-needed sleep.

The minutes ticked slowly by.

In the darkness Bridget stirred.

"Kathleen," came a whisper at last. "I really meant it. I don't want to go without you."

"You may have no choice," Kathleen responded without turning over. "Madam gives the orders."

––––––––

As Kathleen lay beneath the blankets, the even breathing of Bridget telling her that the younger girl was asleep, her troubled thoughts would not allow her the luxury. "What will I do? What will I do?" her brain kept repeating. The posting she had seen that morning suddenly intruded on her thinking.

"If I only had two good legs I wouldn't hesitate for a minute," she dared to think. "Surely my situation in the Americas couldn't become any worse than it is here."

But even as she entertained the thoughts, she wasn't sure of her bold statements. Maybe there were worse situations. At least she had Bridget and Charles and the spoiled young Edmund. At least she had a roof over her head and a warm bed at night. At last sleep claimed her in spite of her troubled thoughts.

Morning came all too soon, and Kathleen was reluctant to climb from the warm bed and stoke up the fire in order to make the breakfast porridge.

She was busy in the kitchen when the door opened and Madam herself appeared. She was enveloped in a warm, new-looking robe, her cheeks void of their usual rouge and her hair wrapped in bits of rag curlers.

"I know you must be wondering about your circumstance," the older woman began without preamble. "You have two choices. I don't wish to dictate your fate. After all, you are not my child." *Nor my responsibility* hung unspoken but unmistakable in the air between them. She hesitated ever so slightly.

"If you wish to come with us to the countryside," she continued, "I'm sure we will be able to find some position for you as household staff. You are quite useful in the kitchen.

Mr. Withers would be willing, I am quite sure, to accommodate a—a family serving girl."

The words stung Kathleen but she held her tongue.

"Or—if you wish to remain in London—you have your job. No doubt the baker will allow you to continue to work for him."

Kathleen still said nothing—just stirred the porridge round and round with the heavy wooden ladle.

The woman muffled a yawn. "There," she said, as if she had discharged all obligations. "It will be up to you." Then she turned and started from the room.

"I feel particularly weary this morning," she said as she left. "I won't be up for breakfast. Have Charles bring my tea and porridge to my room."

Kathleen continued to stir—looking deep into the porridge pot as though searching for an answer to her problem.

———

Her feet slowed as she walked by the posting, but she did not intend to stop. She knew the words by heart anyway. "Ladies! The opportunity of a lifetime."

Her eyes glanced at the words as she moved to pass by. Then she hesitated. Had it indicated anything about when one must decide? She stopped just long enough to glance over the words one more time to try to catch a date. She saw none.

Just as she moved away, a man stepped suddenly into her pathway. With a startled exclamation, Kathleen stopped.

"Are you joining our adventure?" he asked her in an accent Kathleen could not identify.

"Sure now, and what adventure are you speaking of?" Kathleen responded hesitantly, her voice lilting with her Irish tongue.

"Why, going to America, Miss—just like the sign says. Wonderful opportunity. Wonderful. And only a couple passage tickets left. If you want one you—"

"No," said Kathleen, shaking her head nervously. "No, I'll not be wanting one."

The man stepped forward and reached out a hand to tip her face toward the light from the lamppost. Kathleen felt a moment of panic.

"It's a shame," he said candidly. "A face as pretty as yours would be welcomed in America."

Kathleen angrily twisted away from his hand. He seemed to sense her annoyance.

"Pardon, Miss," he said, but his words and his tone contradicted each other. "I didn't mean to offend—just wished to see your face more closely."

Kathleen stepped back, her Irish temper quickly cooling.

"I thought you might be interested," the man went on as though to excuse himself. "That's all."

"And if I am?" The words had left Kathleen's mouth before she even knew she would say them.

"If you are—then come into my office and we'll talk about it."

"I'm lame!" Kathleen spat out, her anger flaring again. "I'm lame. No man—even in the Americas—would wish a lame bride, and that's the truth now."

But the man seemed not to notice her angry words. Instead, he studied her flushed face and sparkling eyes, and a smile crossed his features.

"Why don't you come in for a minute and we'll—"

"I'm a cripple!" she shouted at him again, and moved to pass the man. "See for yourself, sir," she flung back over her shoulder. And she began to clump her way, exaggerating her limp in order to convince the man.

"And what's a little limp?" the man called after her. "In America we allow people to be—different. We are all lame— in one fashion or another."

Kathleen wheeled to give him a piece of her mind, but she saw that he was not teasing her. His face looked serious. His hand was stretched out to her. Her rage subsided in spite of herself.

She stopped, swallowed, and took a deep breath.

"And when does this ship sail?" she asked almost in a whisper.

"In a fortnight" he answered.

Kathleen held her breath.

"I already have nineteen fine young women like you signed for the voyage. I need two more to fill the offers I have from America," the man continued in an encouraging voice.

"Nineteen?"

"Nineteen."

Kathleen could scarcely believe that nineteen young ladies had already laid their futures in this man's hands. Had the short, plump girl called Erma joined Peg in adding her name to the list?

"I'll think it over," she faltered. "Perhaps—"

"There's no time for thinking," replied the man. "I was just coming out to remove the poster. It takes some time to get all the proper papers in order. Anyone sailing on the ship will need to be signed up today."

"But I—" began Kathleen.

"What is it that gives you doubts?" asked the man.

"I know nothing about—"

He interrupted her, "If you are concerned about the gentleman that you will marry upon your arrival in America, let me assure you that they all have been carefully reviewed and selected. Each one is a law-abiding, proper citizen, well respected in his community and well able to provide, in fine fashion, for his—his bride."

Kathleen began to shake her head again.

"And if you fear that you would be rejected over a simple little limp, you do the men of America a grave injustice," he continued. "They are much more sensitive than that, Miss. The true person is found within. In America, we are quite willing to look past the—outer person."

Kathleen noticed his eyes remained on her face as he spoke. He seemed pleased with what he saw there. She wondered momentarily if his words carried truth. Was he really looking past the outer person—or just past the limp that carried the person along?

"I—I'm late for my work," she said simply.

"If you wish to sign—I'll hold the place for you until tomorrow morning. If you stop by tomorrow, I can get right on with the paper work and we should still be able to get you to America."

Confusion swirled about Kathleen. He was offering her a chance to go. He was saying that her handicap didn't matter. He was giving her passage away from the dark, cold streets of London. He was releasing her from being a servant to her own kin. She swallowed, then nodded mutely.

"Tomorrow morning?" asked the man.

"Tomorrow," agreed Kathleen, and she turned and hurried off down the street. She would be late two mornings in a row. The baker would be furious—and it would be all Kathleen could do to keep from responding to his temper. She would have to bite her lip and swallow back the words that she wished to use in response. Her job, her few pennies in wages, would depend upon it.

Chapter Four

Settled

Donnigan allowed Black his head on the trip to town. He felt strangely agitated by Wallis's report. The man really seemed to believe that he was able to order himself a wife. And from where? And who would she be when she arrived? Donnigan had never heard of anything so foolish. Wives came after the courting of lady acquaintances. You spotted one that was pleasing to you and went about wooing her. Donnigan didn't know too much about women, he conceded, but he knew that much. No self-respecting woman would allow herself to be purchased like a catalog item. And no self-respecting man would order one up like—like a new plow.

But Wallis was serious about it all. He was busy selling from his stock in order to raise the money. The prank had already gone too far in Donnigan's thinking. Didn't the fellas who started it, perhaps harmlessly enough, realize that a lonely man was often gullible and beyond reason?

Donnigan hoped he could keep his agitation well in check as he dealt with the situation. It was cruel to take advantage of a man in Wallis's position. Donnigan knew. Hadn't he too felt the pangs of deep loneliness? Didn't he know what it was like to have no one to share his dreams—his home? A man would do almost anything—within proper bounds—to fill the big, aching void in his life. And out here, miles from real civilization, there simply were not many women to be wooed.

Should one actually show up, she had her choice of the whole neighborhood of men and, most often, picked the one with the most coins in his pocket.

Donnigan knew that some of the young men around the area traveled to a city to find their mates. It was one thing if the man—or his pa—was a rancher with lots of hands around to see to the place while he was gone. For a farmer, it was different. Donnigan worked on his own—no hired hands to help with the farm chores or the planting. It wasn't possible to just pick up and head off to the city for the purpose of finding a wife. Wallis was in the same situation. Donnigan couldn't really blame the man for feeling desperate.

But surely *no* wife was a better situation than the *wrong* one, Donnigan reasoned, and if there was a smattering of truth to the rumor that one could just up and order one— wasn't it possible, even likely, that a person could end up with the wrong one?

Donnigan shook his head and put his heel lightly to the black's side. The horse responded gladly, whipping up dust as his hooves pounded the dirt roadway.

It was in this same dark mood that Donnigan confronted Lucas Stein. He had made inquiry and been told that the little man was busy in his office at the hotel. Donnigan shook the dust from his clothes the best he could and went in search of the man.

His knock on the heavy oak door brought a gruff growl, "Come in." But when the man lifted his head from the ledger and saw Donnigan before him, his scowl disappeared. "Harrison," he greeted. "Come in."

The change of tone was not lost on Donnigan. He did not regard the man as a friend in particular, but they got on well enough.

"Howdy, Lucas," he said, hoping that his tone held none of the agitation he was feeling.

"Sit down. Sit down," offered Lucas, indicating a dark leather chair. Donnigan did not have to cast aside broken bridles or other clutter. Lucas kept his office fastidiously.

Donnigan lowered himself slowly to the chair and wondered if he should spend time in small talk or just blurt out the reason for his trip to town. Lucas helped him decide.

"How're your crops doing?"

Donnigan's attention was easily diverted to his farm. He recalled the ride of the morning and his pleasure in seeing the crops grow taller and more mature by the day. He thought again of his herds and couldn't hide the glow in his eyes or lilt in his voice.

By the time Lucas had asked all the right questions and gotten Donnigan's enthusiastic responses, the men had conversed for some minutes.

"There are times I wish I had taken up farming," said Lucas, and Donnigan thought that he sounded sincere. "It would be so much more enjoyable to count calves and foals than spend my time adding up these miserable columns in this ledger." Lucas gave the ledger pages a disgusted flip of his hand.

"Well, a farmer—especially if he's on his own like me—has to keep a few ledgers, too, if he wants to keep things in order," Donnigan assured him and thought again of his reason for being there.

"Yeah—I reckon," Lucas responded. "Be a much better world if one wasn't so tied to balancing the books." He sighed.

There was a moment's pause and Donnigan judged it to be a good time to voice his concern.

"Stopped by to see Wallis," he said, and watched carefully for a response from Lucas. "He's in a big hurry to raise some money. Offered to sell me a couple of his young sows."

Lucas nodded, but the expression on his face did not change.

"Seems to have the notion that—that—well, he seems to have the misunderstanding that he can order himself a wife," Donnigan finished hurriedly and watched Lucas closely.

The man sat toying with the pencil he held in his hands. His head came up and he looked straight at Donnigan. "No misunderstanding," he said flatly, his expression still the same.

Donnigan felt his pulse beat faster. He willed his annoyance to stay in check.

"He thinks you told him that he'd just have to raise passage money and send off for one," he continued in an injured tone.

Lucas looked back down at the pencil. "Didn't he show

you the paper?" he asked calmly.

"What paper?"

"The newspaper with the advertisement."

Donnigan remembered then that Wallis had mentioned a newspaper, but in his excitement he had not produced it nor had he said anything about an advertisement.

"No." He shook his head.

"Well, it's right there in the paper," went on Lucas.

"Then someone has prepared a—an elaborate hoax," declared Donnigan hotly.

"No hoax. I checked it out thoroughly. It's all quite true and legal," said Lucas calmly, rolling the pencil back and forth in his hands.

"Now just one minute," declared Donnigan, leaning slightly forward. "Are you trying to tell me that the paper says you can send off for a wife just like Wallis told me and—and just order one in?"

Lucas nodded. "Something like that," he replied.

Donnigan's hand slapped down on his knee, making the dust lift and drift in a little cloud in the otherwise spotless room. He did not apologize, though he did feel a measure of regret.

"You order one? Like a—a piece of—of merchandise?" The thought was incredulous.

"Now just hold on, Harrison," said Lucas, and for the first time his eyes held some emotion. "It's not like you're making it sound."

"Then what is it like?" asked Donnigan, his face flushed.

Lucas laid aside his pencil and leaned forward. "It gets awfully lonely on the frontier," he explained as though he were talking to a child. Donnigan stirred restlessly in his chair, an expression of disgust and annoyance threatening to escape his lips.

"We need wives. We deserve a wife just as much as the next guy. But where do we get one? I don't know about you, but I'm not about to head off to the city to pick me up some painted dance-hall girl. I want a real wife. One who will be a fitting mother for my children. One who will be around to share life—not one who flirts a little bit and will run off with the next guy who comes along."

"And how do you know—?" began Donnigan.

"How do you ever know?" cut in Lucas.

Donnigan knew that Lucas had read his mind—was ready with the answer to his unasked question. How did one ever know if a marriage would be a good one? One that would bring happiness to both partners?

Donnigan took a deep breath and leaned back in his chair. For a moment the two men sat in silence, eyeing each other coolly. Then Donnigan asked his last question. "And the women—what about them?"

Lucas straightened in his chair, but his face did not flush as he again looked straight into Donnigan's eyes.

"They come out of need—mostly. For some, adventure. Or because they wish to better their circumstances. And we aren't fooling ourselves. Some of them come hoping to marry a rich man. But regardless of why they come, no one coerces them. They come voluntarily—of their own free will."

"You say 'they come' just as though—as though it has been done over and over," Donnigan observed.

"It isn't new, if that's what you're thinking. Many young women, and a few older ones, have already come to America as wives for—for the many men who would otherwise not—not have one."

"And it works?" Surprise edged his voice at this unheard-of method for finding a wife.

"Very well—in many circumstances. I checked it out myself."

Donnigan should not have been surprised. Lucas was not a man to plunge blindly into any new venture.

Donnigan straightened his broad shoulders and agitatedly tapped the fingers of his right hand on his leg. He shook his head slowly, but the fire was gone from his eyes, his voice.

"I don't know," he said at length. "It just doesn't seem right somehow."

"Don't judge too quickly—or too harshly," the man behind the desk said, reaching for his pencil again. "It is simply a matter of two people—both with needs—taking advantage of circumstances to meet the needs of both."

"You really see it—" began Donnigan.

"I really do," the older man assured him. "I could sit here and wait until I'm an old man—and never have a family of my own. Or—" He flicked the pencil in his fingers and let the sentence hang in midair.

Donnigan rose slowly to his full height. He lifted his hat from the floor where he had tossed it and turned it round and round in his hands.

"So you think Wallis is right to get himself a wife—?" began Donnigan.

Lucas nodded. "He has as much right to happiness as the next fellow," he answered evenly.

"But his place is—"

"I know," said Lucas. "Maybe she'll clean it up."

"But it's not fit—" Donnigan started.

Again the man interrupted. Donnigan wondered if he had been allowed to finish one sentence since he entered the room.

"They try their best to match the young woman with the man," Lucas said quickly. " 'Course, there are no foolproof ways of doing that. But they try. And if a man has special requests—he is free to express them when he applies."

Donnigan stood, hat still circling his hands. For one brief moment he was tempted to ask Lucas what kind of woman he had requested, but he swallowed the words. It really was none of his business. Instead, he nodded and placed his hat back on his head.

"Well," he said honestly. "I still don't like the feel of it all—but you've put my mind at ease all the same. If Wallis is—"

"Donnigan," cut in the other man and his voice was low and confidential. "You're still a young man with lots of years ahead to meet and marry—if the right girl happens to come along. But there aren't many girls in this town. I know that and you know that. On the other hand—you might just happen to get lucky."

He stopped and fiddled with the pencil, then looked straight at Donnigan. "Wallis and I are getting on. There won't be many more chances."

He stopped and tossed the pencil aside again, then shifted his position in his leather chair. "But there might not even be as many chances for you as you'd like to think." His voice lowered and Donnigan had to strain to hear. "I happen to know they aren't all spoken for—yet. If you were smart, you'd think about it. It only takes passage money and a small fee to the broker."

Broker? Was that what they called him? Donnigan winced.

"I don't think—" he began.

"Gonna be a long, cold winter," Lucas remarked, lifting his eyes from the ledger sheets and studying Donnigan coolly. "If you change your mind—come see me. Could be a real answer to some woman's prayer."

Donnigan turned and left the room. *Answer to some woman's prayer, indeed. What a self-righteous way of looking at peddling human life.*

He didn't even step into the hotel dining room to have himself a decent meal as he usually did when he was in town. He was too worked up. Too riled. Instead, he headed for the bank to withdraw the money to pay Wallis for the two sows, stuffed the money in his pocket, and went to get his horse.

As he mounted the black his thoughts were still dark and brooding. He turned the horse toward home and gave him his head. He knew the horse would want to run, and he figured a bit of wind in his face might serve to blow away a few cobwebs. Cool his agitation some.

At last he reined in the stallion and coaxed him to settle for a fast trot.

"We'll be home soon enough," he told the horse. "No use winding you."

He wished now that he'd stopped in town for a good meal. He was already feeling hungry, and he hated the thought of getting out the frying pan when he got back to the house. He was sick of salted pork and fried beans. He was sick of tough biscuits and stale coffee. Maybe he was just sick—he didn't know.

————

He stopped by Wallis's to leave off the money. The man grinned his pleasure as he reached for the coffee can stuck inside the fireplace chimney and added the dollars to his stash.

"Got it all now," he said, showing the gap in his front teeth. "I'll hustle it on into town first thing tomorrow."

Donnigan found himself wondering just what kind of woman Wallis had "ordered."

"When do you want me to pick up the sows?" he asked to shake his mind free of the nagging thought.

"I'll bring 'em on over. When ya wantin' 'em?" asked Wallis—but he was still smiling to himself.

Donnigan could hardly wait to leave, but he replied as evenly as he could, "I don't have a pen and farrowing sheds ready. I can work on them tomorrow. Should have them ready in a day or two."

"Friday? Ya be ready by Friday?" asked Wallis.

Donnigan nodded. He should be ready by Friday for sure.

"I'll bring 'em over on Friday, then. Seeing I can get into town tomorrow and take care of everything—I won't need to go Friday."

Donnigan had never seen the man so excited.

"Just think of it," Wallis said as he carefully recounted his money. "The ship will have her over here this fall. Fact is, it leaves next week, if I remember rightly."

"Do you—do you have any idea—who it is that you're—you're getting?" Donnigan didn't know if he had worded his question right, but he could tell Wallis wanted to talk about his plans.

"Sure do," said Wallis with another wide grin. "Sure do. Got her name and all the particulars right here."

He pulled a worn piece of folded paper from his shirt pocket and spread it out on the table.

"Name is Risa. Pretty name, don't ya think? Risa—can't say this next name."

For one moment Donnigan wondered how the man who could not read even knew that the name was Risa. Though perhaps he had been practicing the single name after being told what it was.

Wallis passed the paper to Donnigan. "See fer yerself," he said.

Donnigan turned his eyes to the sheet. Her name was Risa, all right. It gave her last name too, but Wallis had been right. It was a difficult one to figure. Donnigan made no attempt to pronounce it.

"Tall—five feet six inches. Blond hair, blue eyes. Pleasant disposition. Likes children. Good housekeeper. Excellent cook. Good seamstress. Likes to garden. Likes animals." The description ended, and as Donnigan read the last words he lifted his eyes to the shining face of the man before him.

"Pretty good, huh?" Wallis prompted.

Donnigan could only nod. She sounded too good to be true. *Perhaps,* he found himself thinking, perhaps she *was* too good to be true. Maybe all the descriptions of the new wives-to-be said the same positive things.

But Donnigan did not voice his questions. He did not want to dampen the spirits of the other man.

"Sounds real good," he said again, folding the paper and passing it back to Wallis.

Wallis was still smiling.

Donnigan cast one look of apprehension around the untidy small cabin. Risa sure had her work cut out for her. He shook his head and started for the door.

"See you Friday," he tossed over his shoulder.

He was about to step through the door when Wallis called out to him. He turned. The older man moved across the cabin floor and joined him in a few quick strides. "Iffen—" he began. "Iffen you'd like to get yer name on thet there list—I'd be glad to help ya out some iffen yer cash-short just now."

The words surprised Donnigan. Wallis had just sold him two sows to pay for his own "purchase," and here he was offering to help his neighbor so he wouldn't be left out.

"Thanks. Thanks, Wallis," he managed to stammer. "I think I could handle the passage money if—"

"Then ya really outta be thinkin' on it," said the other man. "Fella don't get hisself a chance like this every day."

Donnigan nodded and moved out the door.

He unsaddled his mount and gave him a good rubdown, made sure the trough had plenty of water, and measured out the oats before he turned to the house to fix his own supper.

He had never enjoyed the cooking chores at the best of times, but tonight they rankled him more than ever. He rattled pans and stomped around the kitchen. The fire was out and he was in no mood to rebuild it. He ended up eating some dry biscuits and cold beans. It all tasted like sawdust in his mouth.

He lit the lamp and picked up an old paper that lay on the floor by his chair. He wished he had remembered to purchase a more up-to-date version while in town, but he hadn't even thought of it. He'd already read this one over and over. There was nothing new or appealing on the inked pages. He ended up tossing it into the corner in exasperation.

He took a brief walk around the farm, hoping that the time under the clear sky and evening stars would help to settle him down.

It didn't work. The fact was, the more he thought about it, the more he realized how lonely his life had become. Maybe the other men were right. Maybe there was nothing wrong with getting a bride in such a fashion. Was it really that different from picking one out and going about trying to convince her that you were the man for her? Could you really know what people were like until you lived with them? Weren't even courted women full of little surprises—some good, some maybe not so good?

Donnigan went to his bed. He tossed and turned and fretted and stewed. It was almost morning before he swallowed his pride and made his resolve. Come daylight he would saddle Black and head for town. He would draw out the passage money, sign his name to the proper papers, and wait for the late September ship to arrive.

Chapter Five

No Turning Back

Kathleen stood on the deck of the *Barreth Lily* and watched the land she'd called home for more than a dozen years slip from her view. She had thought that she would be glad to see the last of it, but she was not. Her emotions were in turmoil, and her whole being yearned to slip from the ship and return to what she knew. Even though she had not been happy with her situation, it was all she had ever known.

But as Kathleen watched the shoreline fade into the morning mist, she went over for the umpteenth time the events of the last few days.

The baker, whom she had viewed as always angry and upset and berating her for not hurrying faster, selling more rolls and pies, being too frail to carry the proper-sized load, had suddenly become snivelling. "If it's more pennies ya be wantin', stay and I'll raise your take," he had declared, shocking Kathleen with his pronouncement.

She just shook her head slowly. "The arrangements are all made," she said firmly. "I can't change my mind now."

And Madam, whom Kathleen had expected to be relieved that the girl would no longer be her concern, had ranted and raved. It was apparent that the woman had really expected her stepdaughter to concede to being a member of the house staff at the new country home.

"What am I to do?" Madam had kept wailing. "Not one

staff member of my own to bring to the marriage. How do I know if the others will properly receive me? How do I know if they will carry out my orders the way I wish?"

Then she had turned on Kathleen.

"You are most ungrateful," she had accused, the tears welling in her eyes. "After all these years of giving you a home and shelter—and you reward me in this fashion. How could you? You—you are a most—most unreasonable, unworthy *wench*!" She had spat out the last words, seeming to strain to find something bad enough to say about the slight girl who stood trembling before her.

Only Bridget had been genuinely sad to see Kathleen leave her. "I shall miss you dreadfully," she had said through unchecked tears.

"And I you," replied Kathleen, holding the young girl close. And Kathleen's tears had trickled down her face and fallen in the younger girl's tumbling hair.

"You will write?" Bridget had begged.

"As soon as I have an address to send you," Kathleen had promised.

Bridget had pulled back and studied Kathleen's face, the shock showing in her own. "You mean you don't even know where you are going?" she asked in a whisper.

Kathleen had shaken her head. "I signed up too late," she confessed. "There was no time to—to be matched—with an American. But Mr. Jenks said not to worry. He will make all those arrangements once we arrive."

Bridget's face had still reflected astonishment as Kathleen pulled her close one last time and patted her shoulder.

"Sure now, and take care of yourself," Kathleen had managed, her accent heavy with her concern.

Bridget had managed to nod her head as she wiped at tears and then whispered conspiratorially, "When I get a bit older, I'm coming to America too."

Kathleen had stepped back and looked at her sister.

"I am!" Bridget had declared vehemently.

Kathleen had given Bridget one more hug. "I'll be waiting for you and that's the truth of it," she had whispered against the girl's hair.

———

"There you are!"

It was Erma who interrupted Kathleen's thoughts. Reluctantly she turned from the rail to attempt a smile for her newfound friend.

"Are you still watching jolly ol' England?" asked Erma, teasing in her voice.

Kathleen shook her head. "There is nothing to see now but fog," she replied and had a hard time trying to disguise the tremor in her voice.

"Come. We are having a party," invited Erma.

"A party? What—"

"A celebration really. We have all gathered in a small room down below, and Mr. Jenks is serving wine and cheese."

Kathleen felt that she would rather stay where she was, the salty sea wind flecking her cheeks and tugging at her hair, but reluctantly she followed the other girl.

She had been more than pleased when they had gathered for boarding to find Peg and the robust Erma chatting and giggling in their excitement over the new venture on which they were about to embark. She and Erma seemed to respond to each other immediately, and Kathleen was glad to discover that she was to share a cabin with Peg, Erma, and two other girls by the names of Nona Paulsen and Beatrice Little.

It was crowded, for sure, but Kathleen was glad for the companionship, at least until she made some adjustments to leaving behind everything that was familiar.

Now she allowed Erma to take her hand and lead her hurriedly along the ship's polished, slippery planks. They went down a short flight of steps, took a turn down a narrow hallway, a right into another hall, a few more steps, another hall, up five steps, and again a right. Kathleen was beginning to feel dizzy.

"Wherever are we going?" she asked breathlessly.

"This is a special occasion," laughed Erma. "Mr. Jenks has reserved a special room. This is not where we normally will take our meals."

"I should hope not and that's for sure," responded Kathleen. "I would never find it a second time."

Erma laughed. "You'll get used to the ship," she promised. "They are all laid out generally the same."

Kathleen was surprised. "You've sailed before?" she asked the girl, who was still tugging her forward.

"My father was a captain," Erma responded. "He used to take us with him on some of his trips. I think he just couldn't bear to be away from Mum for that long."

"It must have been exciting," panted Kathleen.

"Aye. It was. I loved the sea when I was a girl." Then her voice lowered and her demeanor changed. "And then I hated it," she declared.

Kathleen stared at her wide-eyed.

"It took my father," said the girl, her voice flat—empty.

"I'm—I'm sorry," breathed Kathleen.

Laughter rippled out into the dark narrow hallway and led them the rest of the way to the celebration party.

The whole small room seemed to be filled with swirling skirts and raucous laughter. Mr. Jenks and a few waiters were the only gentlemen present. Kathleen looked about her in stunned silence. Here were the ladies addressed in the posting. Many ladies. Tall ones, short ones, plump ones, thin ones, dark ones, fair ones, young ones and, surprisingly, a few rather old ones.

They were not all pretty. They were not all well dressed. They were not even all well kept. But they all did appear to be celebrating.

As the two girls stood back, taking in the scene before them, Peg stepped from a cluster of laughing women, waved a hand that held a glass of sloshing liquid, and called rather loudly, "Over here. Join the party."

Kathleen held back but Erma pulled her forward. "Come. Let's join the fun."

Someone passed Kathleen a glass filled with—something. She took a tentative sip, didn't like it, so just held the glass in her hand and tried hard not to look too uncomfortable and conspicuous.

"I thought Mr. Jenks said about twenty girls," she managed to whisper to Erma.

"Twenty from England. The other twenty have joined us from the Continent."

"From the Continent? Mercy me!" exclaimed Kathleen.

"Many of the American men came from the Continent," Erma explained carefully. "They wish wives from their home countries. Only makes sense."

Kathleen nodded. She supposed it did make sense.

She hardly had time to think about it before a shout was heard over the din. "Here's to America," someone called, lifting her glass high in the air. More shouts followed. The party seemed to be getting more and more rowdy.

"Here's to the men," came another cry.

"Here's to their wealth," called a third girl with a hiccup and a giggle, and such a commotion followed her words that Kathleen could hardly think.

Mr. Jenks stepped forward then. Kathleen wondered if he intended to get control before things were entirely out of hand.

"Ladies!" he called. "Ladies!"

It took several cries before he made himself heard.

"Ladies. I wish I could ask you to take a seat," he smiled at them. "But as you can see, there are no chairs available."

"No problem!" shouted Peg, waving her glass in the air, and she plopped down on the carpeted floor, her skirts swirling out around her.

Giggles followed as one by one the women took her lead and settled themselves unceremoniously on the floor. Kathleen stood, her glass clutched in white-knuckled fingers, her eyes wide with shock at the scene. Never had she observed such unruly conduct.

"Ladies," said Mr. Jenks again. "I know you are all excited about this new adventure. And it *is* exciting. I wish you all the very best as you begin your new lives—in a new home—with a new—" He stopped and raised an eyebrow, then smiled at them all, "—husband," he finished, and was rewarded with loud cheers and lifted glasses.

Mr. Jenks had to wait further for the commotion to subside.

"We will be at sea for a number of days. I have a cabin located on the lower deck. It is easy to find, and I have posted my name on it in big letters. I will wish to see each one of you individually during the trip to make all the final arrangements.

"Many of you already have all of the particulars about the man you will be marrying, but a few—"

Mr. Jenks was forced to wait while the cheers filled the room again. Some girls pulled forth papers from hidden spots, like pockets, wrist purses, and bodices, and waved them in the air as they hooted. Kathleen even saw one girl raise her skirts and withdraw a paper from her stockings.

When the calls subsided, Mr. Jenks continued. "You will all need to see me. I will post a list with your name and the date and time that you are to appear. Please, try to keep the appointment. It will be most difficult to reschedule and could put your situation in jeopardy.

"You all have your room assignments. I know they are crowded but"—he stopped to smile—"you have good mates. We will do all we can to make the voyage as pleasant for you as possible.

"Now, I do have many duties to see to, so if you will excuse me. Please, feel free to stay and enjoy yourselves as long as you wish. The gentlemen here will be glad to serve you. And will show you back to your cabins, should you need assistance." He surveyed the group one more time and then added, "Good-day."

Mr. Jenks bowed and left the room to the cheers of the women.

Kathleen stood looking about her. Many of them were still on the floor. Some were even playfully rolling around, their skirts carelessly flying about them. Kathleen felt a little sick. Was this the kind of girl who "sold" herself to a man in America? *Whatever had she done?*

Her face blanched pale and she reached out to clutch Erma's hand.

"I—I'd like to go to the cabin," she managed to whisper. "Could—could you show me the way?"

Erma looked at her and her gray eyes widened. "Are you sick?" she asked anxiously.

"I—I think so," responded Kathleen. "I—I—"

But Erma waited no longer. She took the glass, still filled, from Kathleen's hand and set in on the table. It was promptly grabbed by another hand even before Kathleen could turn away.

Gently Erma led Kathleen toward the cabin. She did not rush. Kathleen had no trouble keeping up to the other girl as she limped along beside her.

"Here we are," said Erma as she opened the cabin door with the key she withdrew from her bodice. "Just you lie down, lovey, and get some rest. The feel of the sea is strange to some. I grew up with it—so I never give it a second thought."

"It's not the sea," responded Kathleen before she thought to check her tongue.

Erma's face showed concern. "Something else, then? Do you have a sickness that you didn't confess?"

All the girls had been grilled about their health.

"Oh no," quickly responded Kathleen. "I'm fine—truly. It was just—just—well I'm not used to such—such bawdy behavior. I—I—"

"Oh that," said Erma with a careless shrug.

"It was—was—oh, Erma, is that the kind of woman they expect us to be?"

"Now don't you go judging too harshly," said Erma firmly. "It's all—well, it's just a—a cover for their real feelings."

Kathleen could only stare.

Erma reached out a hand to give Kathleen a boost up on to her bunk. It was too close to the cabin ceiling. Kathleen felt as if she would soon be gasping for air, but she tried to calm her unsettled nerves. Erma sat down on the lowest bunk opposite and studied her hands in her lap before lifting her eyes to Kathleen again.

"We—we might not have come from the best—best circumstances," Erma began, "but at least we knew where we fit. Now—well, now everything will be different—new—rather—rather scary. For all of us. Oh, we know where we are going. The name of some unknown town. We know if we are to marry a farmer or a rancher or a hotel owner or—" She stopped and shrugged.

"We have been given a piece of paper with a name on it. Maybe a little information. Height, weight, age, coloring. Maybe not even that. But what do we really know? Does he have a temper? Is he quite sane? Will he make unheard-of demands? Use his fists? Drink too much?"

Kathleen drew in her breath. She had not thought of all those horrible possibilities.

"But Mr. Jenks said—" she began.

"Mr. Jenks is a man out to make a profit," Erma reminded her.

Silence hung heavy in the room as Kathleen absorbed that observation. If she had felt sick before, she felt doubly so now. She rolled to her side on the narrow bed and put her hands over her face.

"I'm not out to scare you, lovey," went on Erma quickly, "but we've all had to face the facts."

Kathleen began to sob quietly, her thin shoulders trembling against the worn gray blanket of the bunk.

Erma stood to her feet and crossed to the younger girl.

"Why did you sign on?" she asked quietly.

"Because—because Madam, my stepmother, was marrying again. She didn't want me—or so I thought. Turned out she did. Would have taken me as a housemaid. Oh, I should have gone. I should have," sobbed Kathleen.

"But you didn't have it so good, did you now?"

"No-o. No, it wasn't good," admitted Kathleen.

"Then you did the right thing. The man you wed might be—might be just the man you've dreamed of."

"I haven't dreamed of any man," sobbed Kathleen.

"Then you are a strange lass for sure," responded Erma with a shake of her head.

"Madam always said no man would want me with my limp," said Kathleen, wiping at her tears.

"Such utter nonsense!" exploded Erma. "Why, your limp is hardly more than a little tip. And with your pretty face. Why—I've already seen the deckhands givin' you the eye."

Kathleen could not believe the report. She waved the words aside with a slender hand and tried to sit up, bumping her head on the overhead planks of the cabin.

"Why did *you* sign up?" Kathleen asked, her hand rubbing her head.

"Told you—lost the captain at sea. There was a mix-up over money. We found we'd lost all else too. Between the two grieves, Mum couldn't—well, she just gave up. I lost her, too. I was alone—and well—Peg—I met her at work. She sort of took me in. Talked me into joining—and here I am." She shrugged her shoulders.

"But Peg—" began Kathleen and quickly checked her tongue. She didn't wish to criticize Erma's friend.

"She's drunk," said Erma flatly. "Don't think she's used to drink and she's just overdone it a bit. She'll come round."

Kathleen nodded.

"Truth is, it's all a means of bracing themselves a bit," went on Erma.

"Bracing?" asked Kathleen.

"Oh, I know they talk big—wave their glasses and cheer—but there's not a one of them that isn't just a bit nervous over what she's doing, and that's the way it really is."

Kathleen nodded slowly. She was beginning to understand.

Chapter Six

Preparations

In the days that followed his signing up and turning over the passage money, Donnigan had many moments of extreme doubt. There were times when he sharply berated himself and declared himself to be a silly fool to have fallen for such a ridiculous scheme.

But always when he returned to his cabin at the end of a long, tiring day, he found himself thinking of how nice it would be to be met by a warm smile, a few cheery words, and a plate filled with something hot and palatable for his supper.

It was at those moments that he could not keep himself from whispering under his breath the count of days until the ship should anchor in Boston Harbor.

He got through the haying season. He was glad for the heavy labor that sent him home so tired at the end of the day that he scarcely thought at all before he succumbed to sleep.

He had a few days of rainy weather and restless pacing. And then finally he was into the harvest season. He hoped with all his heart that nothing would happen to slow him down. But it did. More rain showers. Donnigan found them hard to endure and was almost jubilant when he heard a horse approaching and looked out his kitchen window to see Wallis tying up at the hitching rail.

Donnigan was at the door before the older man had a

chance to take a step toward the house.

"C'mon in," he called eagerly. "C'mon in."

Wallis advanced on the house, talking as he came. The man's usual chatter sounded good to Donnigan.

"This foul weather. Ain't good fer man nor beast. Here I was fixin' to have my harvest all in before thet there ship brings my lady—and then this here."

Wallis had turned from saying "Risa" and had begun to refer to the woman as "my lady." Donnigan smiled to himself. He hadn't even dared to think of his ordered bride so possessively as yet. For one thing, he still didn't know one thing about her. Not even her name. It would have been nice to have a name.

"I just got me going good—cut the west field and was hopin' fer sun—" kept on Wallis. Donnigan paid little attention. He pushed the door shut and turned to the stove as soon as the man entered the kitchen.

"Sit yerself," he interrupted. "I'll put on a fresh pot."

While they waited for the coffee to brew, they talked of farm matters.

"Thet second sow farrowed yet?" asked Wallis.

"She sure did. Got a nice litter. Six—plus a born dead. Got one runt in the bunch, but he's doing okay," replied Donnigan.

"Not a big litter—but a fair start," observed Wallis.

"Yeah. It's okay for a first one. She should do better next time."

Wallis knew the first sow had presented a litter of seven piglets—all healthy and of good size.

"They should be good sows," Wallis commented. "Came from good stock."

Donnigan nodded as he poured the coffee and took the two mugs to the table.

They sipped in silence for a few minutes and then Wallis spoke again. "Heard who yer gettin' yet?"

Donnigan shook his head.

Another silent spell.

"Must be kinda hard to wait," observed Wallis.

Donnigan nodded. "Yeah," he admitted at last. "A little."

"I been doin' a bit of fixin'," went on Wallis to Donnigan's surprise. "Ya know—when ya look at a place as a woman might—ya see it a little different."

Donnigan nodded. He hadn't even thought to look at his place through a woman's eyes. It looked just fine to him.

"So what're you doin'?" Donnigan asked his friend.

"Well, I put glass in thet there winda in place of the oiled paper."

Donnigan nodded. He had always wondered why a body would bother to have a window you couldn't see out of.

"An' I patched the roof. Rain ain't comin' in at all now."

Wallis stopped to take another long draft from the coffee cup.

"I figured how I might put up a few hooks on the wall," went on Wallis. "Ain't a place to hang bridles or nothin'."

Donnigan nodded. His bridles all hung on pegs in the barn.

"Might even put up a shelf or two," went on Wallis. "Kinda stack up the dishes and food stuff so thet they don't need to sit on the floor."

"Sounds good," said Donnigan with another nod.

"Figure I'll have it all fixed up fer her," Wallis concluded, looking real pleased with himself.

They played a game of checkers to help pass away the long hours of the rainy day, and Donnigan fixed pancakes and pork gravy for their supper. It was dark by the time Wallis retrieved his old Willie from the barn where he had been taken out of the cold rain and fed his supper.

Donnigan hated to see his friend go. He sure hoped the sun would be shining again on the morrow.

———

Donnigan began to take stock of his own cabin. Though it was sturdy and basically neat for a bachelor, he soon realized that it wasn't exactly the kind of home that would bring pleasure to a woman. He felt panicky. He didn't know where to start or what to do to make it more homey.

He did add a few more shelves and pegs. There would undoubtedly be more things that needed to be put away and hung up after there were two people occupying the premises. Then he went a step further and divided the one big room into two smaller ones. The smaller room at the east end became a bedroom with some privacy and the larger room was the living-kitchen space. Donnigan felt proud of himself for thinking of the idea. He even cut another window into the east end so that the bedroom would have a window all its own.

It was hard getting the job done. Donnigan was back at the harvest again with the weather cooperating quite nicely. His evenings, when he would have wished to put his feet up and rest his back a bit, were spent instead working on the changes to the house.

But even when he got the jobs completed, he still felt uneasy. The house still looked like just what it was: a bachelor's quarters. Donnigan finally gave up. When it came to frills and gingham, he was out of his element.

He did take a look at the yard. He had thought that he kept it fairly neat. Now he could see that what he thought of as neatness might also be seen as clutter. He went to work moving the woodpile a ways from the door, stacking it neatly in a long row against the back fence. He filled in a few holes that had been made by the sows when they had escaped their pens one day while Donnigan had worked the fields. He even thought of constructing a fence, but there wasn't time for that.

"It needs—it needs something," he admitted as he stood back and squinted to get a full look at the house and yard before him.

He wasn't sure what was missing, but he felt the picture he was getting was rather bleak and dull and desolate. He tried to go back in his mind to other houses he had seen in his younger years. His memory brought forth white picket fences and rose bushes in full bloom.

"Can't fix that," he said to himself, but, still dissatisfied, he shifted about to look at the house again.

At last he went to a shed and withdrew a spade. All along the path to the house and the wall by the door, he turned up the fresh soil and shook the grass roots from the dirt.

When he had finished his spading, he headed for the meadow behind the house. He had noticed many varieties of wild flowers there and considered some of them to be quite pretty.

He was disappointed to find that many of the prettier ones had finished their blooming season, but he went to work on what he found.

The transplanting was not easy. He had to trek back and forth, back and forth, one small plant after another held on the shovel surface so that its roots would not lose the dirt around them until it reached its new abode.

He was almost done with his task, gently patting another small plant in place while the sweat traced streaks down his dusty face, when a voice spoke directly behind him. Donnigan had heard no one approach and the voice startled him and brought him upright on his knees.

It was Lucas who stood beside him. Donnigan felt the color rise in his tanned cheeks. He opened his mouth to explain what he was doing, then closed it again. Lucas would have to be a fool not to see for himself.

Donnigan rose slowly to his full height and swatted the dust from his knees with the pair of work gloves he retrieved from the ground.

"Howdy, Lucas," he said, hoping that his voice held more warmth than he presently felt. "Didn't hear you arrive."

"You were busy," observed Lucas, and Donnigan wondered if he saw a glint of amusement in the other man's eyes.

"Thought the place looked rather bare," Donnigan offered in embarrassed excuse. "Don't want her shocked by the drabness of it all."

Lucas made no reply to Donnigan's remark. He was carefully studying one of the small plants that Donnigan had just placed along the walk. "Where'd you get that one?" he asked simply.

"Down by the crick," replied Donnigan, rather pleased that he had found such a pretty little cluster of flowers.

"What is it?" asked Lucas, bending down to get a closer look.

"I don't know—but it was blooming and I thought it—that a woman might think it rather pretty."

"Maybe it's a weed."

Donnigan straightened his shoulders and looked at the other man evenly. "I might not know the first thing about flowers—but I've made it my business to know weeds," he replied evenly.

Lucas rose to his feet again and nodded in concession.

"Come in," said Donnigan, moving toward the door. "I'll put on the coffee."

"Can't stay," said Lucas, and Donnigan hesitated.

"Wire came today," said Lucas. "The ship's in."

Donnigan whirled to face the other man. Suddenly he felt like a small boy waiting for the Christmas that finally arrived. It was all he could do to keep himself from tossing his hat in the air and giving a loud whoop. He restrained himself and gave a slight nod instead.

"Wallis know?" he asked as calmly as he could. He looked at Lucas and was surprised to see the undisguised glow in the other man's face.

"I'm stopping over there soon as I leave here," Lucas replied.

Donnigan swallowed hard. Never had his emotions played such havoc with his normally calm demeanor. He shifted his feet uneasily, feeling that he would surely burst at any minute.

"It'll take 'em a couple weeks to get here," Lucas continued. "They'll catch the train from Boston—then connect with the stagecoach the rest of the way. Jenks says he hopes to have them out here week from Saturday."

A week from Saturday! Donnigan's thoughts raced. After waiting for weeks—months—it suddenly seemed so soon and yet so long until he would actually be meeting—seeing for himself the one— He couldn't even think about it. It made his heart race.

He shifted again.

"Well, I'd better get on over and tell Wallis," Lucas went on. "He's right anxious."

Donnigan swallowed again and managed to nod his head.

Then Lucas reached into his inner coat pocket and withdrew a piece of folded paper.

"Here's the name of the lady you're to meet that Saturday," said Lucas casually, and Donnigan held his breath as he accepted the sheet. He felt a cold sweat encase his body, and he took a long, deep breath to steady the pounding of his heart.

He had to say something. Anything. Just so that Lucas wouldn't think him a complete fool.

"Suppose you've known your lady's name for weeks," he managed.

Lucas nodded his head. Took a step toward the team that waited where they had been tethered to a tree in the lane. Then paused and said simply, "It's Erma," and then walked away—but not before Donnigan had caught the excitement in his eyes.

Donnigan watched the man leave and then went in to put on the coffee. He knew that Wallis would be over just as soon as he got the word.

He was very conscious of the paper in his shirt pocket. He wanted to seize it quickly and pore over its contents— and yet could not bring himself to touch it. That little slip of paper—the name that it bore—was going to change his whole life.

He stoked the fire and filled the coffeepot with fresh water and poured in a handful of grounds before he allowed himself to sit down at the kitchen table and reach a trembling hand to the breast pocket.

"Name—Kathleen O'Malley," he read aloud and stopped to let the name roll over his tongue a few times before his eyes crinkled in a smile. He liked it.

"Twenty-one. Dark hair and brown eyes. Lots of experience in cooking and keeping house." That was all.

Donnigan read the paper again and again. He wished there were more—something to give him some—some indication of just what kind of person Kathleen O'Malley was. Was she tall? Short? Sullen? Cheerful? Did she like horses? Hogs? Would she want a garden spot? Hens? Was she—? Donnigan carefully folded the bit of paper and replaced it in his breast pocket. He sighed deeply. He guessed that he should be happy to have her name. At least he could step forward come the important Saturday and say, "Good-day, Miss O'Malley. I do hope your trip wasn't too exhausting."

The coffee began to fill the room with its steamy aroma, and Donnigan moved to shift it farther back on the stove.

"One thing for sure," he murmured, surprising even himself. "I hope she's not sulky and silent. I couldn't stand that. I don't want to have to still talk things over with Black once she gets here."

And Donnigan moved restlessly to the window to see if Wallis was making an appearance on the country road. He did wish the man would hurry.

His eyes dropped to the flowers he had just planted.

"Those are for you, Miss O'Malley," he said softly, and it gave him an odd sense of connection. He felt his cheeks warm. But he could not help himself from continuing—from changing his little statement. "For you—Kathleen."

The name felt new and strange on his tongue, but somehow, in the saying of it, Donnigan felt a stirring of sweet possession.

Chapter Seven

Passage

The troubles on the Atlantic crossing began on their second day out. After the raucous celebrating by the band of women on board, a time of illness followed. Kathleen could have felt that it served them right, but as she observed their intense suffering, she could feel only pity for them as they held their heads and groaned with each roll of the ship. It kept both Erma and Kathleen running to empty the chamber vessels and wipe the brows with cool wet rags.

By the time the women were once again on their feet and ready to take to the decks for walks in the open air, the winds became brisk and the ship began to toss and roll. Even Kathleen had to take to her bunk. Erma was the only one in the little band who did not become seasick.

At long last the storm subsided and the women began to stir and search for fresh air. The cabins were so small—so crowded—that even on the good days the air became stale and close. But on the days of the illnesses, Kathleen had often wondered if she would be able to endure. She longed, at times, for the cold, damp streets of London, where she could at least draw a breath of fresh air.

Though she became acquainted with many of the women heading for America, she really only learned to know well those who shared her own cabin and her own dinner table. She soon discovered that even though they shared the same future destiny, they were varied and different in their per-

67

sonality, background, and outlook. Some of the opinions expressed shocked and horrified the young Kathleen. She found that more and more she chose to walk alone about the decks or share the time with Erma rather than be a part of the chatter of the other women.

Many of the women from the Continent she did not get to know at all. The fact that some of them spoke very little English was of course one factor—but there were other differences, though Kathleen wouldn't have been able to put her finger on them.

"Some of them are farm women," Erma had explained, "and shy."

Kathleen had never lived in the country—at least since she had left Ireland at the age of two. Her father had spoken of the farm. To his dying day he did not cease to grieve that he had lost family property at the time he had fled his country. Always his dream had been to return—to reclaim; and though Kathleen knew nothing of the circumstances, she claimed his dream as her own after he had been taken from her.

"Sure now—and ye're an O'Malley," he used to tell her. "Ye've nothing to be ashamed of and plenty to be proud of, so hold yerself tall. And maybe someday—when God himself rights the wrongs in the world—ye'll get back what truly belongs to an O'Malley."

Kathleen wished later that she had asked more questions. Talked more to her father of his beloved homeland. Now, as the ship bore her to America, she reasoned that she would never have opportunity to see the land of her own roots again.

Perhaps other girls were grieving over lost homelands as well, for as the days passed, tempers became short and occasional disturbances erupted. One ended up in a hair-pulling duel, and two other girls were found rolling around on deck, skirts flying along with screams of obscenities. Kathleen had never seen anything like it—not even in the streets of London where such things were said to occur.

And then there was the girl from the Continent who

changed her mind about going to America after taking up with one of the deckhands aboard ship. The whole incident was rather scandalous, to say the least, and Mr. Jenks had a good bit to say about it.

Kathleen waited impatiently for her appointment with Mr. Jenks. She noted that she was the last name on his posted list. It didn't surprise her. After all, she had signed up very late.

However, she was not ignored. Several times during the voyage the man sought her out. Once he even invited her to his cabin to share his dinner. Kathleen was uneasy about the invitation and sent word that she was not feeling well—which, because of the tossing sea at the time, was no exaggeration.

Still he continued to seek her. It began to be noticed by the other women, and Kathleen found herself the butt of crude jokes. From henceforth she tried her hardest to avoid the man as much as possible.

———

As they neared the end of the journey, anticipation ran at fever pitch. Kathleen walked about the deck, enjoying the brisk wind that reddened her cheeks and whipped her hair. But even as she wished solitude, she felt drawn to the others as she heard their high-pitched, excited voices. She drew near to a noisy group in time to catch a comment.

"The marriage ceremony comes first," a tall, bony-looking girl was declaring. "I'm not putting one foot in the door until I hear the words. No fallin' into *that* trap. I'm not leaving it so he can show me the door again if it suits his fancy."

"And I'm telling you, I won't stand for one minute of tomfoolery," a big girl named Mary added. "I didn't come all this way to be somebody's serving girl."

A few girls hooted in agreement.

"An' I don't plan to be slopping pigs—even if I marry a farmer!" shouted another.

"No. Nor a milkmaid, either," called Peg.

"I'll cook—providing, of course, he gives me the makings," said a brassy older woman with a painted face and tinted hair.

"I'm hoping for a man rich enough to provide a young wench or two to help with the house chores," ventured a woman with blond hair piled haphazardly on the top of her head.

There was another shout of approval.

"Tell you one thing," a short, stout redhead said as she lifted her skirt to hike up her hose. "If I don't like what I find—I'll not be stayin' long."

A chorus of agreement followed the comment.

"And what will you do, lovey?" asked another.

"Aye—don't you worry none about Rosie. She can handle herself," replied the redhead with a wink of her eye and a toss of her skirts.

Kathleen moved away. "Marriage is a permanent thing," she argued to herself. "One doesn't pull out just because there are a few more household chores than one had hoped there would be." The whole conversation disturbed her.

Right then and there Kathleen made herself a pledge. She would stay with this arranged marriage no matter what it turned out to be. She would make it work. She would. She had agreed to it and would stick to her agreement.

She walked away from the shifting, chattering group and sought the stinging sea breezes to blow her discomfiture away.

She jumped at a touch on her arm, then saw that it was Erma who had joined her.

"Don't pay no attention to 'em," Erma said close to Kathleen's ear so that the wind wouldn't whip the words away. "It's all just nerves and bravado. We're all getting a little tight strung."

Kathleen nodded. She was certainly tight strung.

"Most of 'em are good, clean, hard-working girls who've never been away from home before. They're scared to death and that's the way it really is."

Erma moved closer to Kathleen and the smaller girl took comfort in her presence.

"Let's walk around to lee side so we can talk out of this wind," Erma suggested, and Kathleen followed with no hesitation.

They found a small bench sheltered from the wind and took refuge, wrapping their shawls tightly around their shoulders for warmth.

"There now," said Erma, giving Kathleen a forced smile, "this feels better."

Kathleen nodded, watching the rise of distant waves and feeling the pitch and roll of the sea.

"We'll be docking tomorrow," said Erma. "Have you seen Jenks yet?"

"In the morning," replied Kathleen.

"He sure has held you off," observed the other girl. "Yet at the same time, he's been almost courtin' you the whole passage."

"Courting?" echoed Kathleen. She had not felt courted— only harassed.

Erma nodded. "Why do you think the teasing from the others? They noticed all the attention. The 'How are you? Can I get anything for your comfort? Would you join me for dinner?' " Erma chuckled softly at Kathleen's shocked look.

"I don't think—" began Kathleen. Something about Mr. Jenks made her feel dreadfully uncomfortable. But she couldn't put it into words. Not even to Erma.

"Well, no matter," went on Erma briskly. "We're almost there now. Not much chance for courtin' from now on, is there?"

Then, to Kathleen's relief, Erma changed the topic. "See all the gulls? That means we're getting near land."

Kathleen lifted her face and studied the birds circling overhead. She could hear their cries and it awoke some deep, distant memory. Had their Irish farm been by the sea? Then her thoughts were interrupted as Erma spoke again.

"So you still don't know—?" she began, then stopped, knowing that Kathleen would be able to finish the question.

Kathleen shook her head. "Sure, and the suspense is givin' me goose bumps, and that's the truth," she answered with a shiver.

They sat in silence for a few minutes listening to the cry of the gulls and the swell of the seas.

"If you could wish—and have it come true—what would you wish for?" asked Erma softly.

"That he be Irish," responded Kathleen with no hesitation.

"And his trade?" asked Erma.

"I wouldn't care. He can be anything—just as long as he—" She didn't finish her statement.

"And what would he look like?" asked Erma, seeming to enjoy her little game.

Again Kathleen did not hesitate. "Dark wavy hair coming down at the sides with curling sideburns, with laughin', teasin' eyes, and a dimple in his chin." She had described her father just as she remembered him.

"I'd like a tall blond rancher with broad shoulders and a straight nose and even teeth with a—just a small, carefully trimmed mustache," laughed Erma.

"Oh, Erma!" cried Kathleen, laughing too, and then adding in sudden anguish, "And what do you think *they* are hoping for in us?"

Erma shrugged, then answered thoughtfully, "Companions. Cooks. Housekeepers. Someone to share laughs and—and trials. Someone who won't nag or chatter too much or complain over wet firewood or footprints across the kitchen."

Kathleen shivered.

"At least—I'm hoping that's what he'll want. I could be that, Kathleen. But if he wants more—then . . ." Erma let the sentence slide away to join the cry of the gulls and the sighing of the wind.

Kathleen reached for her friend's hand.

"The biggest wish of all"—her voice was a whisper—"is that you will be wherever I am, and that's the pure truth of it," she said with feeling.

Chapter Eight

Meeting

The next morning Kathleen went promptly for her appointment. Mr. Jenks rose to meet her as she entered the room and took the liberty of using her first name. "Kathleen," he beamed, taking her arm and steering her to a chair placed a little too close to where he himself had been seated. He reclaimed his chair, so close to Kathleen that she feared they would bump knees. She drew back in her seat as far as she could.

"And are you feeling quite well now, my dear?" he asked solicitously.

Kathleen assured him that she was fine.

"You are such a delicate little thing," he said smoothly, "that I feared for you on this arduous journey."

"I'm stronger than I look, sir," Kathleen responded a bit curtly.

He nodded and changed the subject. "We dock this afternoon."

Kathleen nodded her head.

"I was hoping that we would have some time to—to enjoy each other's company on the voyage, but the heavy seas—"

Kathleen shifted uncomfortably and broke in. "I'm anxious to hear where I'll be going, sir," she dared to say.

"Oh yes." He came back to attention and placed his hands on his knees. "Well—that, my dear, is still a matter of concern for me, as well."

Kathleen did wish that he would stop calling her his dear.

"As a matter of fact," he went on, "it has still not been decided."

Kathleen frowned.

"Oh, never fear," he said reaching to take her hand. "You will have a place, I can assure you. Even if I have to take care of you myself." He winked and grinned and Kathleen felt terribly annoyed.

"Why am I here?" she asked boldly. "Why make an appointment just to tell me that there have been no arrangements?"

"There *have* been arrangements," he said, and reached to give his mustache a twitch. "I would like you to take dinner with me tonight at my hotel. I'm staying at a rather elegant place downtown. I think you will like it. Perhaps without the tossing of the sea we will have better opportunity to—"

"That is unthinkable," said Kathleen, standing to her full five feet two inches. Her face flamed with her disgust. "I will stay with the others—wherever they are staying."

His face grew dark with anger. "You are a proud one, aren't you!" he spat at her. "And after all I've tried to do."

"Sure now, and I was of the impression that my passage was paid by an American gentleman," Kathleen reminded him heatedly.

"Yes, Miss," said the man, his anger now matching her own. "And he shall have you—pity him, whoever he is. I wouldn't want to deal with such a temper every day for the rest of my life."

Kathleen spun on her heel and left the room.

"Stay with the others," he called after her. "I want you around to take the orders of where you are to go."

Kathleen didn't answer. She needed to get into the wind to cool off her hot cheeks.

But she would be there when it was time to find out where she would be going. And she hoped with all her heart that it was a long, long way from Boston and Mr. Jenks.

———

There was much commotion when the ship finally pulled in and docked in Boston Harbor. The women milled around, squealing and shouting and clutching belongings. Kathleen crowded close to her cabin mates, her dark eyes big, her face pale. As crowded as the cabin had been, she wished for just a few more days of feeling secure there.

Their names were called out and they walked the gangway by groups of four. As her feet touched the firm dock, Kathleen nearly lost her balance. Erma, close beside her, giggled.

They were all placed into carriages and taken through the streets to a large hotel. It felt strange to be back in a city again. Kathleen noticed that it was much newer, much cleaner, than her familiar section of London. She wondered if it would be possible for her to stay on here. She felt a drawing to this new American city. A feeling that she might soon be able to "belong" here.

But the very next day they were called to a drawing room where Mr. Jenks presided.

"Ladies—we are about to the end of our journey together," he informed them as though this were a matter of deep sorrow to all. "You will be heading west—to one point or another. From here to Chicago you will share a train. There you will be met by a gentleman by the name of Mr. Henry Piedmont. He will give you your final tickets and send you on the last leg of your journeys. From Chicago on, you will be fanning out and heading in different directions—though still westward.

"I do wish each of you every happiness in your new land—and your new unions."

He bowed low and gave them one final grin, smoothed his mustache, and then said firmly, "Miss Kathleen O'Malley—you will need to see me for final instructions."

He turned on his heel and was gone.

All eyes seemed to fix on Kathleen. She straightened her shoulders, lifted her chin, and followed the man from the room.

He must have expected her to do just that, for he went

only a few steps beyond the door and turned to wait for her.

"This way," he said with a nod of his head, and Kathleen obediently followed him.

They crossed the hall and entered a small room, and he motioned toward a chair and turned to lift a sheet of paper from his pocket.

"Before I hand you this," he said, looking straight at her, "might I say that I am a tolerant man. I am staying on in Boston. I am quite willing to forget your outburst of last evening—should you have changed your mind."

For one moment Kathleen frowned, not understanding his words. When the truth finally dawned, she rose quickly from the chair, her face flushing, her eyes flashing anger. Without one word she reached out and snatched the paper from his fingers before he had a chance to react.

"You may be sorry, you know," he called after her as she moved from the room as quickly as her limp would allow.

Kathleen did not return to her room immediately. She had to find some privacy before she dared look at the paper she held. At last she found a chair tucked in a rather dark corner of a distant hall and dropped onto it, trying to still her anxiously beating heart.

Carefully she unfolded the bit of paper.

"Donnigan Harrison," said the paper. "He is a late signer like yourself. Not much is known of him. I hope you will not be sorry."

Kathleen crumpled the paper in her hand and then felt immediate remorse. Carefully she placed it on her lap and tried to smooth out the wrinkles. She would need that piece of paper. It was all she had.

"Donnigan Harrison," she repeated. Then her eyes lit up. She wasn't really familiar with the surname, but Donnigan did sound rather Irish. For the first time she felt some hope.

———

The train ride was long and stuffily hot. Kathleen had thought the boat trip had been difficult—but at least then they had enjoyed the crispness of the ocean winds. Not given the luxury of berths, they were crammed together in seats with hard straight-backs and no place to put their tired heads. The long nights were spent in restless shifting to try to find some way to relax tired bodies.

At last they reached Chicago. Kathleen may have been interested in studying the city had she not been so totally exhausted.

The man called Piedmont was on the platform when they arrived. As they stepped off the train, he rounded the women up and hustled them to a side room, much like herding cattle, and grinned at the group nervously as he called out names and passed out tickets. Kathleen had not felt particularly close to many of the women, but as she sat and watched group after group being hurried out to catch this coach or that train, she felt panic tighten her throat.

At last her own name was called along with a number of others, and she stood up and walked numbly past the man and accepted the ticket along with its instructions of where to go and how to get there.

She was more than a little relieved to look around her and find that Erma was also in the group.

But Peg was gone. As were Nona and Beatrice. There were just Erma and her and four other women whom she didn't know well. All four were from the Continent. She wondered if they spoke English. They seemed so shy and frightened. Kathleen moved closer to Erma, drawing some assurance from the presence of her friend.

Quickly they compared sheets and found to their relief and excitement that they shared a common destination. With excited cries they threw their arms around each other and wept unashamedly. It would be so wonderful—so *wonderful* to know someone, to have a friend in the new, strange land.

Soon they had boarded another train and were chugging their way out of the station. Though still not given a berth, they were not so crowded. By now they were so weary that Kathleen felt they could have slept almost anywhere.

She was right. The girls from the Continent fell asleep almost as soon as they boarded the train, the oldest of the group soon snoring loudly.

Kathleen did not stay awake to see if it annoyed other passengers. She rolled up her shawl against the coolness of the window, laid her head against it, and fell asleep.

She was stiff when she awoke in the morning, but at least she felt somewhat better.

"And how long are we to be on this train?" she asked Erma.

"I'm not sure. Someone said three days."

Kathleen winced. She was so tired of travel. Travel and heat and people and dust. It seemed that it all went together in America.

———

After the train came the stagecoach, which they met in a small, dusty frontier town of gray wooden buildings and gray wooden boardwalks. The sign at the post office indicated that it was Raeford. Kathleen felt that they must be going to the end of the world. She had given up craning her neck to look out the window. There were so many miles of the same thing. She did find the herds of deer and antelope and buffalo rather exciting. She had seen no such animals on the back streets of London.

But for the most part, they rode in silence. There was really very little to talk about.

When they reached a small station by the name of Sheep's Meadows, one of the girls from the Continent was separated from them and sent in another direction on another stage. Kathleen could sense the girl's panic. She felt her own hand go out to grasp Erma's. She was so thankful that she would not be going off all on her own.

Later, two of the other girls were sent off in another direction. Kathleen wondered how far they would travel before they were separated again.

There were still three of them when the stage pulled into

Aspen Valley. They all looked at their sheets of paper one last time. They were home.

————

Donnigan wished he had made arrangements for Wallis to ride along with him to town. He could have used some support. Never in his whole life had he felt so nervous—not even when he had been treed by a big grizzly or the time he had been thrown in the path of stampeding cattle. Somehow he had managed to escape those perils. It seemed there was no escaping this one.

He cast one last glance around his snug cabin. All the dishes had been washed. Even the pots. They were all stacked carefully on the shelf beside the stove. He had made his bed rather than just tossing the blankets up to cover the pillow. He had even used a scrub brush and hot soapy water on the floorboards. Things looked pretty good.

He moved from the room and closed the door firmly behind him. As he walked the dirt path toward the barn and corrals, he studied his makeshift flower garden. He had lost only one of the plants that he had brought from the meadow. But only three were still blooming. Still, it was better than nothing, he reasoned.

He would have loved to show up in town with the black. Everyone around admired the magnificent horse, and Donnigan couldn't help but feel that the big stallion would make some kind of favorable impression.

But the black hated the harness, and Donnigan knew that he could hardly ask his new wife to climb up behind him and be toted back to the farm cowboy fashion. Then there would be all the trunks and cases that she would have with her. No, it just wouldn't work to take the saddle horse. Donnigan hitched the team to the wagon and started off to town.

————

The stage was late. Most of the town didn't even notice, but the three men who paced back and forth waiting anxiously for its arrival and trying hard to hide their jitters certainly did.

Lucas, who felt in charge because of having collected the passage money from the other two men, pulled out his gold watch on the long gold chain over and over to study the time.

Donnigan simply checked the sky. The sun was moving on past where it should have been at the proper arrival time. Wallis stomped back and forth, back and forth, spitting chewing tobacco at the end of his boots. Then the three would shift positions slightly and begin all over again.

"Fool driver!" exclaimed Wallis angrily, letting go with another streak of brown stain. "Shouldn't be allowed to fritter away his time and keep workin' men waitin'."

Donnigan had to smile in spite of his own impatience.

"Do you want to come over to the hotel for coffee?" asked Lucas hospitably, but just as he asked the question a cloud of dust appeared in the distance.

With the sighting of the stage, Donnigan really felt his stomach begin to rile up. "This is it! This is it for sure," he said to himself. "There's no turning back now."

Then a new thought struck him. "What if she isn't even on the stage. Maybe she changed her mind or got sick or—"

He felt sudden exultation like he had when he had escaped the bear's long fangs. But only for a moment. He admitted to himself that even though he was terribly nervous about the whole doings, he would be dreadfully disappointed if she did not show up.

The stage rolled to a halt in a whirl of dust. As the three men held their breath, the stage master stepped forward and opened the door.

Out stepped a lady. She was not too tall, rather pleasingly plump and had a slightly nervous yet generous smile. She scanned the three men before her, then looked again at the tall blond man with the broad shoulders and wide Stetson and gave him a special smile. As Donnigan's heart leaped in response, Lucas stepped forward.

"Welcome, Miss—?" he said, lifting his hand to doff his hat.

"Kingsley," said the young woman; her voice was soft and husky with emotion. "Erma Kingsley."

Lucas suddenly looked as nervous as a schoolboy. "You're mine," he blurted, then flushed with embarrassment. "I mean—Lucas Stein here, ma'am." He reached out a hand and she accepted it.

Donnigan was momentarily disappointed, and then his attention jerked back to the stagecoach where another woman was making her appearance. She was tall and a little stiff, her eyes dark and piercing. She straightened to her full height and surveyed the men. Before any of them could make a move she spoke in broken but careful English, "Which of you is the gentleman Tremont?"

Wallis swallowed his chew of tobacco and his face turned deep red. Donnigan wasn't sure if it was the fault of the potent chew or his nervousness over meeting his Risa.

At length he seemed to get hold of himself, but not before the woman had given him a dark, stern look.

"Ma'am," he said and copied what he had seen Lucas do. Only in his great agitation, the hat that he had intended to doff flipped from his shaky fingers and went flying into the dust at his feet. He stammered and stuttered and bent to retrieve it, slapping it on his thigh and making a little puff of dust lift almost in the lady's face.

"Sorry, ma'am," he had the good sense to apologize. She did not look pleased.

Donnigan turned his attention back to the stagecoach door. So far two very different women had descended. If Donnigan could have had anything at all to say in the matter, he would have hoped the third one would be somewhat like the first one.

But as he lifted his head, a little wisp of a thing was descending the steps. Maybe his wife-to-be wasn't on that stage, after all.

The young girl moved slowly toward the little group, and Donnigan noticed that she walked with just the slightest limp. She was a pretty youngster. Donnigan wondered fleetingly if she was the daughter of a local farmer or rancher, but he hadn't seen her around before. Perhaps she was a visiting niece of someone.

Miss Erma Kingsley turned as the young girl neared them. She spoke again in a voice that didn't sound quite as strained now. "This is Miss Kathleen O'Malley," she said evenly, and Donnigan was glad he didn't have a chaw of tobacco in his lip. He surely would have swallowed it just as Wallis had.

Kathleen O'Malley? his thoughts ran quickly. *But she's a child. I—I ordered a—a woman.*

"I guess you must be Mr. Harrison," Miss Kingsley said to Donnigan, "as you are the only one left." She gave him a warm, candid smile and Donnigan found himself wishing again that the fates had been kinder to him. For a brief moment he envied Lucas. Then he turned to the approaching Miss O'Malley and carefully doffed his Stetson.

"Miss," he said and forced a smile. He could hardly address her as ma'am, now could he?

She returned his smile with a hesitant one of her own—and as Donnigan looked into the clear dark eyes, he felt his heart give a little flip.

Chapter Nine

Adjustments Begin

Kathleen had stopped to take a deep breath before disembarking from the stagecoach. Her heart was thumping and her hands felt sweaty. She straightened her bargain bonnet on her dark curls and smoothed the nearly new gloves over her small hands. Her whole outfit had been purchased in Boston as part of the "passage deal." It was simple and inexpensive, but it was new. Kathleen was grateful for that. Her own patched wardrobe had been painfully inadequate.

Now as she paused at the top of the steps and brushed the dust and wrinkles from her skirts, she took one more deep breath. *Please,* she begged whoever was "in charge," *Please let him be Irish.*

There was a little cluster before her when she stepped out. For a minute she stopped and squinted into the harsh afternoon sun, letting her eyes adjust from the dark interior of the stage.

There was Erma, already smiling confidently at a short, well-dressed, bespectacled gentleman who stood with his watch still in his hand as though he were timing something. "Surely he's not," Kathleen murmured under her breath, then quickly switched to, "He must be Mr. Stein." The gentleman was well into his forties, she guessed.

Kathleen's eyes shifted quickly to the other little man who was bustling about, thumping his hat against his leg and grinning rather ridiculously. The stern Risa stood frowning at him—and Kathleen judged that she was looking at another "match." The man was rather ill-kept, but his hair was slicked down and his face shining from a morning scrubbing. Kathleen judged him to be even a bit older than Mr. Stein.

"But I don't see Donnigan," she whispered to herself, and a stab of fear shot through her. Had there been a mistake? Had Mr. Jenks sent her all this long way out west with the name of a man who didn't really exist—just for spite?

Then her eyes looked beyond the two couples and she saw another man. Tall and broad and blond—and looking pained and worried. For a moment she thought she was looking at the very man Erma had described to her on board ship. Surely—surely this was Erma's intended. But no. Erma was already paired.

"Sure now, and he's a—a giant," Kathleen mused, her feet refusing to move farther. Just as she thought of turning and retreating to the safety of the stagecoach, the man looked up, seemed to realize who she was, and smiled. In that one warm, nervous smile, Kathleen saw a reflection of her own feelings. She managed a tentative smile in return—and then he was moving toward her with confidence and more grace than she would have expected from such a large man. Kathleen stepped forward to meet him. One thought was uppermost in her mind. *He's not Irish—and that's the truth of it.*

———

Lucas had made arrangements for them all to take tea together at his hotel. "We need to get acquainted," he'd said calmly to Wallis and Donnigan, and the two men had nodded in agreement. Donnigan had been glad to let Lucas take charge.

Now Lucas cleared his throat, nodded his head to Will, one of his hired hands, and offered his arm to Erma, who accepted it with a slight flushing of her round, dimpling cheeks.

"You must be weary. All of you," said Lucas, letting his glance take in the three women. "It's a long, tiring trip. We will take tea at the hotel."

Donnigan noticed that he didn't say "my hotel," though he could have. Lucas already owned half the little town.

Wallis, who still hadn't put his hat back on his head, self-consciously stuck an elbow out in the direction of Risa. She appeared not to notice.

Donnigan turned to Kathleen. She looked so tiny. So frail. So very young. His immediate instincts were to protect her. He reached to place his hand under her elbow to guide her across the roughness of the town's main street. *She shouldn't be in the West,* he found himself thinking. *It's too harsh. Too rugged. She'll—she'll—*

But she interrupted his thoughts. "Sure now, and I'm glad to be back on my own two feet." Then Kathleen bit her lip, remembering that men do not like chattering women.

He couldn't help but grin. Her accent was so thick that he had to concentrate to catch the words. She sure did talk cute.

He did have presence of mind enough to offer, "How long have you been traveling?"

It was Kathleen's turn to strain to untangle the strange-sounding words. My, he had an odd accent. She had never heard one speak in that manner before. He sure wasn't Irish.

She shook her head. She still felt nervous—almost to the point of being giddy, but she controlled her voice the best she could and replied softly, "I'm not sure." The "r" seemed to roll on her tongue. "It seems forever. The ship—then the train—then this here fancy cart." She nodded her head back in the direction of the stage, and Donnigan would have laughed except he saw the seriousness in her little face.

They reached the hotel and followed Lucas, who led the way with Erma. Donnigan could see the eyes of the three women carefully scanning the interior. It was really quite a nice hotel for such a small town. But then, Lucas did everything in splendid fashion.

The little side room was especially ornate. Donnigan

found himself wondering if Lucas had carefully redone it for just this occasion. He heard Erma exclaim "Oh, my!" as her eyes surveyed the room and a smile deepened the dimples.

Risa slyly took in the room in one quick glance, and Donnigan wondered if he hadn't seen her eyes light up briefly.

But it was Kathleen who captured his attention. He heard her quick intake of breath and saw her dark eyes widen as they quickly scanned the room. Pleasure and wonder seemed to eminate from her very being. Some word escaped her lips, though he wasn't able to catch it because of her heavy accent.

She likes pretty things, he observed, and it pleased him. Then he thought of his own plain cabin. Certainly there were no plush draperies, brocaded settees, ornate wallpapers, or thick carpets there. Stirrings of concern tightened his throat again.

But Lucas was inviting them to the linened table and nodding toward the side door to a waiter who stood ready to give the signal to the kitchen staff.

Donnigan was surprised by the whole affair. He had thought he knew Lucas. Now he realized that he really did not. It became clear that the man had class far more befitting an eastern city than their little town. He was refined, gentlemanly, almost suave. *He sure must have been studying his books or practicing somewhere,* Donnigan observed silently. *He sure didn't learn all this around here.*

The truth was, unknown to any of the town folk, Lucas had spent considerable time in careful research and preparation for the event. And he had practiced, night after night, in his own suite of rooms until he felt he would be totally comfortable in his new role.

Wallis, Donnigan's closest neighbor and friend, suddenly stood out as crude, cocky, and terribly unsophisticated. His lack of refinement had never bothered Donnigan before, but now as he watched him stumbling his way clumsily through a simple, rather feminine ritual like afternoon tea, Donnigan couldn't help but wonder what Wallis's Risa was thinking.

But to Donnigan's further surprise, the three ladies at the table seemed just a bit nervous and unsure as well.

Perhaps they are just tired out, he thought to himself.

"I'm sure our American customs are a bit primitive compared to your European ways," Lucas observed with a smile, "but for today, will you grant us the privilege of serving you? In the future, you may serve the tea."

That eased some of the tension around the table. Lucas took over the duties of both host and hostess, and the women seemed to relax.

Lucas tried to draw out his guests, addressing each of the women by turn. Donnigan noticed that Erma answered rather easily, dimpling with each reply. Kathleen spoke when spoken to, but her answers were brief and to the point and her words heavily accented. Donnigan observed Wallis frown and wondered if the man had understood one word of what Kathleen had said.

But it was Risa who had very little to say. Her brief replies were curt, choppy, and with no feeling. She, too, had an accent. Perhaps German—or Dutch—or Russian. Donnigan really had no idea. But every time the woman made even a small comment, Wallis grinned as though she had just made a standing-ovation public address.

It was a leisurely teatime, and Donnigan was thankful to Lucas for arranging it. It had helped to break the ice. Perhaps they would all feel just a bit more comfortable with one another. But Donnigan also knew—Lucas had made it clear—that once tea was over, the other two men were on their own.

Lucas had frowned when Donnigan informed him earlier that morning that he wanted two rooms in his hotel. Two rooms. One the best that he had.

Donnigan had flushed, then hurried on to explain. "I figure she—she has a right to one night to think it over—make sure she still—"

Lucas had nodded then. But he still seemed to feel that Donnigan was taking unnecessary precautions.

"I've arranged with the parson for a seven o'clock wedding," Lucas replied. "Then we'll take dinner in my rooms."

Yes, Donnigan thought, *I'm sure you have everything carefully and neatly arranged.*

Now as Donnigan glanced around the table, a strange idea occurred to him. *What if Lucas had been hitched with Risa?* The mental picture almost made Donnigan chuckle. He shifted his big booted feet under the table and tried with effort to wipe the grin from his face before anyone noticed it. But it sure would have been funny—Lucas trying to teach the straight-backed Risa to jump through his hoops.

Donnigan's glance slid back to Erma. Her round cheeks dimpled and her eyes sparkled with trust as she listened intently to whatever Lucas was saying to her. Yes. It appeared that Lucas would have no trouble with Erma.

But what was he doing thinking of the other two men? What would he do with Kathleen? Again Donnigan shifted uneasily. It was a perplexing consideration.

———

Kathleen was awed by the splendor of the town's one hotel. She had never been in a hotel before except for the one in Boston—and it had been rather old and stodgy and stale-smelling. And the girls had all been crowded on cots in a few airless rooms with single dingy windows that looked out on a dirty back alley. Kathleen had not been impressed—but she figured that's how hotels were.

But this hotel was like—was like a rich man's castle, a king's tara, Kathleen concluded—though she had never been in the likes of those either.

She was concerned by the white linen on the table. What if she spilled something? She was confused by the square of white linen near her plate. What was she to do with it? Unsettled by the fine china that looked as if it would break at her touch. Alarmed by the row of forks, knives, and spoons. Why would anyone ever need so many just to take tea?

And when the tea trays promptly arrived, Kathleen gasped. She had never seen so many dainty sandwiches, iced cakes, and fancy tidbits. She didn't know where to start—so she watched Lucas, who began the proceedings by passing the "proper" item to Erma and unobtrusively indicating the piece of silver that was needed. By following the flushed Erma, Kathleen felt that she could not go too far astray. She began to relax and enjoy the afternoon repast. Like the others, she was hungry. Their fare had been simple and scant for the entire journey.

As she savored the tasty food, Kathleen almost—almost but not quite—forgot the big man who sat beside her. Under other circumstances she would have been very aware of his presence. In fact, she marveled that the food took so much of her attention. In her need for nourishment, she even found herself thinking, *If this is America, I like it.*

But as her appetite was appeased, she found her thoughts returning to other things. Things like wedding vows. Strangers. Separation from Erma. Family back home. Suddenly Kathleen lost her appreciation for the food. Her stomach tied in knots. She pushed her plate back slightly as though she couldn't stand the thought of one more bite.

She cast a glance around the table. Lucas was still talking engagingly with Erma, who listened in rapt attention.

"—my living quarters are right here in the hotel," Kathleen heard him say, and then he quickly added, "I do hope that you don't find the arrangement disagreeable."

"Oh no," dimpled Erma. "It's most—most—pleasant." And her eyes scanned the room again as her cheeks flushed.

Kathleen found her eyes following Erma's. *Wouldn't it be a wonder to live in a place like this,* she found herself thinking.

Kathleen shifted her eyes to Wallis, who ate the sandwiches as though he'd been near starving. One patched elbow rested on the white tablecloth so the hand wouldn't have so far to go to reach the mouth. Kathleen noticed that he had pressed two of the dainty sandwiches together so they would make a more worthwhile mouthful.

Risa sat stiffly beside him. Even her tightly secured bun at the nape of her neck looked offended by the man beside her.

Donnigan sat too close to her for her to see his face. But she surprised herself by realizing that already she had it memorized. She could visualize the intense blue eyes, his most outstanding feature in her way of thinking, the straight nose, the tanned cheeks—one bearing a small scar that made her wonder what had happened—the firm chin with the slight cleft, the blond hair that wished to curl, especially at the nape of his neck.

But he was so big. So big and broad. Kathleen had been used to smaller men. Men more like Lucas in stature. For one brief minute she wished that she could change places with Erma. Erma was the one who had wanted the tall, blond rancher. Kathleen felt dwarfed beside him. Like a—like a small child looking up to her father. She didn't like the feeling. Didn't like it at all.

But Lucas was folding the square of linen that he had placed on his lap. Kathleen saw Erma reach for hers and fold it slowly as well. Kathleen followed suit.

"I'm sure we all have our own plans for the rest of the day," Lucas was saying.

"I have had your luggage taken to my—our rooms," Lucas said to Erma. "I'm sure you would like a bath and rest to refresh yourself."

Erma looked at him appreciatively—and then back to Kathleen. For one brief minute Kathleen saw panic in the gray eyes.

"The—the wedding—?" Erma began.

"Will be at seven," said Lucas evenly.

"I—I was wondering—since I know no one and—and Kathleen is my—my friend, could—could she attend me, sir?"

Kathleen's breath caught in her throat. She hadn't thought of attendants.

For one moment Lucas frowned slightly. He had already made all the arrangements. Then he looked back at Erma and nodded, if somewhat reluctantly. "Of course," he said. "That—that will be—fine."

Lucas turned to Kathleen; then his eyes lifted to Donnigan's. "At the church—at ten to seven," he said, and both Kathleen and Donnigan knew that Lucas meant for Donnigan to be sure to deliver her there promptly.

"I told the parson we'd be on over as soon as we et," Wallis was saying to Risa.

The woman raised no objection, just nodded her head and followed Wallis as he headed for the door, his grin still firmly in place.

"Are you tired—or would you like to walk?" Donnigan asked Kathleen solicitously, nervously fingering his broad-brimmed hat.

He really felt the need to get to know something more about this young girl, and the teatime had not really given them much opportunity to speak to each other.

Kathleen was weary, but she, too, felt the need to discuss their future plans.

"I'll walk," she replied evenly, wondering to herself if Donnigan had forgotten her limp. Would he be embarrassed to be seen on the streets with a lame partner?

They turned from the coolness of the day to the heat of the afternoon sun. Kathleen accepted Donnigan's offered arm. It seemed very strange to be on the arm of a man. She was used to scurrying through the streets of London on her own. Only the "ladies" were escorted.

They walked for a time in silence and then Donnigan spoke. "I have arranged for us to spend the night at the hotel," he informed her.

Kathleen lifted her eyes. She was waiting for him to say when they were to be at the church to stand before the parson.

"I thought you might be too tired to travel on out to the farm tonight—having traveled for so many days already," he went on to explain.

Kathleen nodded silently.

Her thoughts went on, tumbling over one another. *He said, "the farm." I'll be back on a farm. I wonder if one can see the sea?* Kathleen felt sure that they must be close to the sea. They had traveled so far. Surely the land couldn't stretch much farther. She lifted a hand to wipe her hot brow with the white hanky that had been purchased in Boston.

Donnigan stopped short.

"It's too warm for you, isn't it? I'm sorry. You really need to get out of the sun. You should rest."

Kathleen had never heard such concern in anyone's voice before. Certainly not concern over her well-being.

"I'm—I'm fine," she responded.

But he already was turning their steps toward the hotel.

"Your things have been taken to the room," he told her as they entered the cool lobby. He did not add that he had been totally surprised at the scarcity of luggage. The stage driver had needed to assure Donnigan over and over that the one little trunk was "all the luggage that the little lady had."

"I have the key—right here. I'll take you up."

With one hand under her elbow, he ushered her across the reception area and up the carpeted stairs. Kathleen felt woozy. Was it the heat—the events of the day—the man— or—or everything combined? So much was happening. So quickly.

They turned to the right at the top of the stairs and continued down a short hall. He presented the key and turned the lock in the door, opening it wide so she could enter. It was a pleasant room, with heavy blue and gold draperies, blue and gold carpet, and a soft bed that beckoned Kathleen.

"I'll send someone right up with hot water. You can bathe and rest," he assured her, then continued. "I'm sorry you won't have long. We need to be at the church right at ten to seven. If we don't, Lucas will have our hides."

He turned to leave, reaching for the doorknob to pull the door shut behind him.

"Wait!"

Kathleen's little cry stopped him.

"*Our* wedding?" asked Kathleen with more boldness than she thought she possessed.

"Tomorrow," he answered briefly. "Not 'til tomorrow."

He shut the door and was gone and Kathleen stared after him with wide, flashing eyes. Then she tugged a glove from her fingers and flung it on the bed beside her.

"Sure now—an' it's either you or me for the hall tonight, Mr. Donnigan Harrison, sir," she said angrily.

Chapter Ten

Confused Beginnings

As promised, there was a knock on Kathleen's door shortly before seven. She was ready and feeling somewhat refreshed, though she did wish she could have rested much longer.

But it was exciting to be off to Erma's wedding—even with the disappointment that Mr. Donnigan Harrison had chosen to stall concerning theirs. What if he continued to put it off? *What if he didn't plan to marry at all?* Kathleen felt her stomach churn.

He offered his arm, but because of the anger and confusion that still twisted her thoughts, she chose to refuse it. With head held high she limped along beside him, ignoring him as much as it was possible to do.

"Did you rest well?" he asked kindly, and she answered with a slight nod of her head and firmly pursed lips. If he thought it odd, he did not make comment.

He led her down the steps and through the lobby, out into the warmth of the evening and toward the end of the town's main street. Kathleen made no attempt at conversation, and he seemed to be sensitive to her mood.

She spotted the little church set back from the road before he lifted his hand to guide her down the wooden walk.

"Here we are—and on time. Lucas won't need to pace," said Donnigan with a hint of good-natured teasing in his voice.

They entered the church to find Lucas there ahead of them. He was resplendent in a black formal suit with a small rosebud tucked in his button hole.

The man whom Kathleen identified as the town parson stood at the front of the room, book already spread open before him. *It appears that the preacher doesn't wish to keep Lucas Stein waiting either,* thought Kathleen; and in spite of herself, she felt a smile curving her lips.

Erma arrived promptly at seven. She came by carriage, even though the hotel was only a few blocks down the street. Kathleen could only stare. Erma was dressed in white with a lacy veil covering her carefully coiffed blond hair. The dress was a bit tight and Erma appeared to be holding her breath, but Kathleen wondered how the man had managed to be that close in his estimate of size for his new bride. The white-gowned bride carried a bouquet of red roses and white carnations on her arm. Kathleen had never seen anything quite so splendid.

"Your flowers," Lucas was saying, and Kathleen looked from Erma to find Lucas offering her a small version of Erma's bouquet. She accepted it numbly.

A total stranger stepped forward and offered his arm to lead her toward the man at the front. For one brief minute she panicked, wondering if she was being led up to marry this balding, stern-looking gentleman, and then she realized she was simply being escorted up to be a witness to Erma's wedding. She took the offered arm and walked forward, her thoughts quickly scrambling to wonder what had become of Donnigan.

But the parson was already speaking and Kathleen forced her attention back to his words.

"Dearly beloved—" His voice was low and carefully modulated. Kathleen wondered if Lucas had brought him in just for the event. He sounded so proper—so perfect. But she quickly reminded herself that the man belonged to the whole town. She knew Wallis and Risa had made use of his services earlier that afternoon.

With that thought, Kathleen felt her face flush again. So

why hadn't Donnigan made arrangements? Or had he—and canceled them when he saw her lameness? Maybe she was a reject—just as her stepmother had warned.

Kathleen lost total concentration. Before she knew it the man with the book was saying, "May the God of heaven bless your union with His love, joy, and peace. Amen," and she knew that the short ceremony was over.

———

Donnigan was still struggling. He didn't feel any concern about the hotel dinner hour. That he had already arranged for, and it always seemed rather easy to chat over food if one felt that talk was necessary. And he knew that Kathleen was dreadfully tired and would wish to retire early—so that would take care of the evening. But what then? They had to talk seriously—sometime. They were due at the church at ten the next morning. But that hour seemed to be approaching awfully fast. He had a lot of thinking and sorting to do in a short time. He had thought himself prepared—and he would have been—had a girl like Erma stepped forward when the stage pulled into town. But a *child*? What was Jenks thinking of? Surely this—this—bit of a girl should still be at home in her family's care. So what was she doing here—ready to promise herself in marriage? Ready to take on the responsibilities of a grown woman? It didn't make a lick of sense to Donnigan.

He mulled over the problem all the time he waited for Lucas's ceremony to end, but he was no nearer a solution when the last Amen was spoken.

As the couple turned from the altar, Donnigan rose to his feet. He was the only one in the small church except for the parson and the wedding party. He wasn't sure if he should move forward with his congratulations or wait for the new bride and groom to come down the aisle. He waited.

The parson came first, with Lucas and Erma close behind him. With a bit of hesitation, Donnigan stepped forward and extended his hand.

"Congratulations," he said heartily to Lucas. The man, who was usually so composed, couldn't hide the merry twitching of his mustache. He had pulled the whole thing off—he was a married man, his twinkling eyes seemed to say.

Donnigan let his eyes shift back to his own bride of the morrow. She came slowly down the aisle on the arm of Grant Crayford, the town's officious banker. Donnigan had never been particularly fond of the man but had accepted him as a necessary part of the town. Now as the man placed his overly soft hand on the small hand that rested on his arm and leaned down to say something quietly to the young girl, Donnigan liked him even less. It was one thing for him to escort Kathleen, but quite another for him to be so solicitous—so possessive. Donnigan's starched collar suddenly felt too tight. He was a bit too quick in stepping forward and taking Kathleen's other elbow, gently easing her away from the dark-suited man.

"Our dinner is waiting," he said in explanation, and she allowed herself to be hurried away.

As she left the church, Kathleen saw Lucas assisting Erma back into the carriage for the short ride back to the hotel. Kathleen almost felt envy—and then Erma lifted her eyes and met Kathleen's for just one moment.

The gentle smile was still firmly in place, but the eyes shadowed briefly. *She's frightened,* thought Kathleen in that one quick exchange. *She's nervous and frightened.*

Kathleen wished to pull her hand free and go to the girl, but she managed a wobbly smile in return, hoping that it conveyed to Erma some measure of warmth and assurance, and then the carriage door was closed and Erma was gone.

———

Kathleen felt so weary she could scarcely keep herself alert to enjoy the tasty meal that was set before them. Donnigan kept talking and she hoped that she was giving sensible responses.

She was still angry and concerned about the hotel arrangements. She wasn't quite sure how she would handle it when the time came, but she had no intention whatever of sharing a room with a man who wasn't her wedded spouse.

I could sleep right here on this chair, she assured herself, feeling tired enough to do just that. *Or I could curl up on one of those settees in the lobby.*

But Donnigan was speaking again. "I know you are very tired," he was saying, "so rather than talk wedding plans tonight, we'll wait until morning."

Kathleen cast him a distant glance.

"I don't have special clothes," Kathleen admitted, her eyes held to her plate.

Donnigan shifted uneasily.

"Nor do I," he admitted. "Only Lucas would think of all those things."

"Do you mind?" asked Kathleen simply.

"No." His answer was curt. Almost sharp. Then his voice softened. "Do you?"

Kathleen shrugged her slim shoulders. Erma had looked awfully nice. But when it came to the truth, she had never even considered a wedding gown. "No," she said after a moment's hesitation.

"What you are wearing now looks real nice," Donnigan went on. It was the closest any man had ever come to complimenting her. Kathleen felt her cheeks warm.

The meal ended in silence. When they were finished, Donnigan rose to his feet and offered his arm to Kathleen.

"We'd better go up before you fall asleep at the table," he teased gently.

Kathleen longed for the soft bed in the room upstairs. Yet near panic gripped her. Now she would need to stand her ground. Now she—but how—and what would she say?

Donnigan led her up the steps and down the hall and again opened the door with the key. He held it for her to enter, but Kathleen stood rooted to the spot.

"This arrangement isn't much to my liking, sir," she said, her head lifting and her chin thrusting forward.

Donnigan looked puzzled. "Is something wrong with the room?" he asked innocently.

Kathleen's brogue was thick as she tipped her head and answered, "Sure, and the room is fine. It's the company that concerns me."

"The company?" It was clear that Donnigan was confused.

"On this journey I've shared a tiny closet-sized room with more women than I could count," went on Kathleen, "an' it didn't cause me one troubled moment—but sharing so large a room—with a man—now *that* I've no mind to do."

"A man?" Donnigan found himself peering around the door and into the room. His face still registered puzzlement.

"If you count yourself a man, sir," said Kathleen, her voice edged with anger.

"Me?" he asked incredulously.

Then Donnigan began to chuckle softly. "You thought—I mean, you thought that—that. . . ?" He couldn't finish the question.

"We won't be married until tomorrow," he reminded her.

Kathleen just stood and stared, her anger turning to confusion.

"My room is down the hall," explained Donnigan quickly, pointing his long arm with outstretched finger.

With the words he reached out and pressed the room key into Kathleen's hand. "Your key," he said and pulled another key from his pocket. Then he reached up and ran a hand through his blond hair. Kathleen could see the red gradually stain his tanned cheeks. Only the white scar stayed untouched. He licked his lips nervously and fingered the hat in his hand.

"I'm sorry," he muttered. "I didn't mean to cause you concern. I—I guess I didn't explain. I just didn't think. I'm—I'm sorry."

Kathleen felt the air leave her lungs—the anger leave her eyes. She stood for one brief moment trying to get back her control, and then a slow smile began to lighten her face.

"Sure now—and I did make a bit of a scene, didn't I?" she admitted.

He looked steadily into the dark eyes. Unexpectedly his hand lifted to touch the slim shoulder. "I—I'm glad," he whispered. "I'm glad you're that kind of girl."

Kathleen felt a stirring to her very soul. She swallowed hard, managed a nod, and moved into the room.

"I'll knock on your door in the morning," he called softly after her, and Kathleen heard her door close firmly.

Chapter Eleven

A Start

Kathleen had been fearful that once she fell asleep, she would not wake up until the afternoon of the next day. She was so weary from all the travel—all the emotional turmoil—but to her surprise she had a restless night.

First she had a difficult time getting to sleep. She thought of Erma and Risa and wondered how they would adjust to being wives of men they hardly new. She thought of Donnigan, her own man she did not know, and wondered if there were any secrets he was hiding. Indeed, she even wondered if his claiming another room was just a ruse so he might sneak off in the night, leaving her stranded and without means in this western town.

From there her thoughts turned to home. They quickly skipped over her stepmother and her plans for the marriage that would by now have taken place. She didn't even stop to wonder if the woman had found the happiness she had sought. Instead, Kathleen passed on to Bridget, and emptiness seemed to press in upon her. She missed Bridget. It was true that the girl was rather spoiled and undisciplined, but they held a fondness for each other.

Would Bridget be off to school? Yes. They were already into the fall of the year. The young girl would be in boarding school by now. Kathleen wondered how she was doing. Was the bit that Kathleen had been able to teach her standing her in good stead?

Kathleen even thought of Charles and young Edmund. Did they like the countryside? Had they been favored with ponies of their own?

Strangely enough, Kathleen even thought of the cranky old baker. Had he passed on her hawker's basket to another poor girl? Kathleen didn't even want to picture the girl in her mind. The back streets of London were really not a place for a young girl to be.

And over and over, Kathleen's mind went to Donnigan. Once again she said to herself, the disappointment still intense within her, "Sure—he's no Irishman, and that's the truth of it."

But what was he? And who was he? He was fine enough to look at—though his size disquieted her. He said he had a farm. Kathleen felt pleased about that. A farm would be a nice change from cluttered, dirty streets and dark, tall buildings.

He seemed a gentleman—though certainly not as polished and sure of himself as Erma's Lucas. But even as Kathleen had the thought, she stirred uneasily. She wasn't quite sure if she would have been pleased with a man like Lucas. He seemed so intense—so in control—so totally mechanical. Again Kathleen wondered if Erma would be happy.

"I must stop this," Kathleen scolded herself once again. "I will be a rag in the morning and not fit for a wedding and that's the truth of it." But even as she thought the words, Kathleen wondered again if there really would be a wedding.

————

Donnigan retired earlier than he should have. He just didn't know what else to do with his long evening. But he may as well have stayed up and paced the streets. He tossed and turned and thumped his pillow, then wadded it beneath his head and tossed again.

Never had his mind been in such a state. Never had he faced such a difficult decision.

"Twenty-one! That's ridiculous. She's more like—like—

I know what I should do," he told himself firmly. "I should bundle her up and put her right back on the stage and send her home to wherever she came from."

But Donnigan knew that he didn't have the money for a second passage aboard an ocean-sailing ship.

"Maybe someone would take her on as hired help—let her grow up a bit," he thought next. But he quickly dismissed that idea. How would he know if she was properly treated or whether she was taken advantage of?

"Well, I shouldn't marry her, and that's for sure," he told himself. But if he didn't marry her, what would he do with her?

It was quite obvious from the little luggage she carried that she wouldn't be able to financially care for herself.

"Well, I can't just take her to the farm without marrying her," fumed Donnigan. "Even if I slept in the barn."

There just didn't seem to be an answer. It wasn't that he was displeased with her. She was a pretty little thing—and she had spunk. He had seen that firsthand. In fact, when he really thought about it, if he'd had his pick of the three women who had disembarked the stage, he likely would have chosen her. The tall, prim Risa certainly would have made him quake in his boots. He wondered how Wallis was faring.

And Erma, though she appeared to be agreeable and cheery, made him wonder if such a constantly agreeing person might soon get on his nerves. But little Kathleen—when she smiled, her whole face brightened, and when her temper flared, those dark eyes shot sparks. He had a feeling that living with her would be a rather exciting adventure.

But she was so small—so young. He tossed again and in the stillness of the hotel room he softly cursed Wallis and Lucas for talking him into this crazy scheme and then the man Jenks who had no more sense than to send a child in the place of a woman.

He tried to push the disturbing thoughts from his mind so he could get some rest. "Twenty-one!" he snorted in disgust. "Why did she have to go and lie about her age?" He'd have to have a talk with her and sort it out in the morning.

And he did need to ask her to please stop referring to him as "sir." He much preferred Donnigan.

————

Kathleen was up and dressed, her belongings carefully packed, long before the rap came on her door. She knew, with the aid of the mirror, that she didn't look rested, but she figured that she could likely get through one more day on nerves.

Donnigan stood before her, silently fumbling with his hat. Kathleen felt relief in seeing him. At least he hadn't skipped town. She thought he looked as though he hadn't slept so well either.

He managed a smile. "Good morning," he greeted. Kathleen did hope he wouldn't ask if she had slept well.

"I don't know about you, but I sure am ready for some breakfast," he said in his easy manner, and Kathleen managed a smile and a nod. She had been feeling hungry for a couple of hours.

He led the way back to the dining room and placed their orders. Kathleen was glad for the strong, hot coffee. Not only did it taste good, but it gave her something to do with her hands.

"We need to talk," he surprised her by saying. He looked uneasy, but seemed determined to say what he had to say.

"Quite frankly," he began, shifting his big frame on the brocaded chair seat, "I had pictured a—an older woman. One a bit more—more mature. Bigger." He indicated a rough shape with his hands.

Kathleen felt the color draining from her face. It was her limp, she just knew it.

He stopped and Kathleen saw him struggle with what he should say next.

"Your—your—the piece of paper that I got said you are twenty-one." His eyes seemed to challenge her. He hated lies. It had bothered him all through the night that she might be a person that couldn't be trusted. How could you live with a person, sharing your life and your dreams, if you couldn't even trust her?

Kathleen met his gaze steadily. He saw her eyes widen with surprise—then darken with concern.

"It said that?" she asked almost under her breath.

He nodded.

Kathleen's eyes fell to her plate. She shook her head slowly. He thought he could see anger smoldering in the dark eyes when she raised them again.

"It's that Mr. Jenks," she said. "I—I told him my true age—but the man must have put down—I'm—I'm sorry."

The last words were spoken so softly that Donnigan had to strain to hear them. But her eyes spoke volumes. Donnigan was ready to believe that she was sorry, just as she had said.

"I—I don't think that Mr. Jenks is a man to be trusted," she finished lamely and her eyes registered anger once more.

Donnigan shifted his weight again. Suddenly he felt anger himself. Anger toward the man Jenks whom he had never met. He had to move on with the conversation or he would find himself asking questions that he might wish he had not asked.

"Why did you come to America?" he asked her simply. "I mean, at your age—why aren't you still home with your folks in Ireland?"

Kathleen took a deep breath. He had a right to some answers. She had a few questions of her own.

"I came from London," she said first and saw the surprise in his face.

"Sure, and I am Irish. But I have lived in London ever since—ever since my father had to give up his land. My mother died when I was a wee one. I hardly recall her face. My father married again—to a woman from France. Then my father died a few years back. We were left in—in rather—difficult—circumstances. I worked—if you call hawkin' rolls and pies on the streets of London work. And then—then Madam"—the name slipped out before Kathleen had time to change it—"my stepmum, decided to marry again." She

stopped and raised her eyes to his. "So I signed up and—"
She shrugged and looked down at her cup.

Donnigan sat silently digesting all that she had said.

"Why didn't you stay with your family?" he asked softly.

"They were moving to the country," she answered evenly.

"You don't like the country?" He thought of his farm and
little cabin as he asked the question, and a strange fear accompanied the words.

"And I wouldn't know, would I now, not having memories
of my own. But my father always said it's a fine place to be
a livin'."

"So why didn't you move with them?"

Kathleen's eyes dropped again. Her fingers slipped to her
lap where they clasped in agitation beneath the spread of
tablecloth.

At last she raised her eyes again and Donnigan saw hurt
and confusion there. "I wasn't wanted—except as household
staff," she said honestly.

"Staff?"

She nodded, a bit braver now. Her chin came up and he
saw the fire back in her eyes.

"Madam gave me two choices. A member of the household
staff in the country—or a hawker on the London streets."

Donnigan had no comment. He lowered his own gaze and
toyed with the cutlery by his plate. She'd really had no
choice. And neither did he, he decided as he stirred restlessly.
Child or not, there was really nothing for him to do but to
marry her.

They arrived at the small church at ten o'clock. There
was no fancy white gown or formal black suit. Lucas, dark
suited, took his place beside Donnigan. Erma stood at Kathleen's side. They used their slightly wilted flowers of the day
before. Only this time, Erma graciously offered Kathleen her
bridal bouquet. The ceremony was short and direct, and in

a few moments Kathleen looked shyly up at Donnigan. They were now husband and wife.

———————

Donnigan did not really look at her again until they were traveling the dusty, rutted road to the farm on the high seat of the wagon. He wondered just how disappointed she was feeling, having visited Erma's posh hotel suite of rooms before leaving town so that they could bid each other goodbye.

But her face did not look dark and gloomy. She lifted her hand to remove her bonnet and brushed back her straying dark hair. Her face turned into the breeze that rustled the grasses by the roadside, and she took a deep, satisfied breath.

"I've longed for the country ever since I was a child," she admitted frankly, and Donnigan, relieved, took a deep gulp of the fresh warm air.

They rode in silence again, and then Kathleen tilted her head as though listening intently.

"What bird is that?" she asked, her voice expressing excitement.

"Just a wood thrush," he answered.

"You must teach me all the birds," she responded and then seemed to catch herself. She was not to be a chatterer. And she certainly was not to be giving orders. Her face flushed with her embarrassment.

But Donnigan seemed not to notice. "You like birds?" he asked, his voice deep and warm.

"Oh yes," she breathed and then fell silent.

"Would you fancy some hens?" asked Donnigan after a few moments.

"Oh yes," said Kathleen again. She would love hens— and geese—and ducks and—and maybe even— She checked herself again.

"We'll get some—come spring," said Donnigan, and the matter seemed settled.

Kathleen had so many questions she wished to ask. Where was his farm? What did he have there? If there were no chickens, were there sheep? Cattle? She wished he would talk about it. She longed to ask. But she would not make him angry by prattling on while he wished for solitude. She bit her tongue to keep the questions from pouring forth.

At the same time that Kathleen held herself in check, Donnigan was bemoaning the fact of her silence.

We'll never get to know each other at this rate, he thought dejectedly. There were many things he wanted to ask her. Wished to tell her. But she didn't seem interested in conversation. He didn't wish to make her uncomfortable by plying her with questions or to seem boastful by sharing with her about the farm he had carved for himself from prairie sod. But it was difficult to ride along for so many miles in complete silence. He would have been doing more talking if he were riding Black, he decided.

They drew near a small farm and Kathleen felt her heart quicken. Was it their farm? But no, Donnigan made no move to tug on the reins of the horses.

"That's Wallis's place," he said, and Kathleen looked at it with renewed interest. They were almost past when Kathleen spotted Risa. She was in the shade of the small building, bent over a tub of washing. Already a line was filled with clothing that fluttered in the afternoon breeze.

"I see Risa has gone right to work," observed Donnigan with a smile. Kathleen waved, but the busy woman did not look up from her scrubboard.

It wasn't long until Donnigan did turn the horse into a farmyard. Kathleen fell in love with it at once. It was so much better than the dark little cottage along the London street. And it was easy to see that it was much nicer than the farm Wallis and Risa occupied down the road.

But Kathleen bit her tongue and tried not to let her intense excitement show. He already thought her a child. He would be more than sure if she bounced up and down on the wagon seat and clapped her hands at the sight of her new home.

Donnigan stole a sideways look. He hoped to see a sparkle in her eyes—but he saw instead a stoical face and hands tightly clenched in her lap.

Donnigan helped Kathleen down from the high wagon seat and deposited her on the ground. He saw her eyes go to the flower beds that he had labored over on her behalf and for one moment they brightened, but she made no comment.

"I'll bring your things to the house after I care for the team," he told her. "You go ahead on in."

Kathleen hesitated.

"Would you like me to go with you—this first time?" asked Donnigan, almost shyly.

"Oh no. No, it's fine," replied Kathleen. But she did feel dreadfully strange about entering the home of the man, though she knew it must quickly become her home as well.

She lifted the latch on the unlocked door and stepped inside. The kitchen-living quarters were neat and roomy. Kathleen drew in her breath. It was more than she had dreamed of—her own country home. She wouldn't have traded places with Erma for anything in the world.

She moved slowly forward, taking in the small shelves that were stacked with dishes, the big black stove with its copper kettle, the table, chairs, the shelf with assorted books and manly items like belt buckles and a checker board.

At last she dared to venture farther and found the bedroom beyond. So much room for only two people. She and Bridget had been forced to share a room where they could scarcely stand up beside the bed.

Kathleen did clasp her hands. She wanted to dance around the little room, but she thought she heard Donnigan coming. She forced her face to become blank, placed her hands demurely at her sides, and returned to the kitchen just as he placed her small trunk beside the door.

"Is everything okay?" he asked soberly, hoping with all of his heart that she would respond with some enthusiasm.

"Fine," she said simply, with no emotion whatever.

He stood for one minute and then nodded his head. "I'll get some fresh water," he informed her and lifted the pail from its shelf.

After he had left the house, Kathleen did do a little jig around the table. It was perfect. Just perfect. She could be happy here. She knew she could.

She looked about again. "It will be so homey with curtains at the windows, hooked rugs on the floor, a throw over the big stuffed chair in the corner, a few bright—"

But Kathleen checked herself. He hadn't brought her here to totally disrupt his home. If she began to make all of those changes, he would think she wasn't happy with what she had. He would think her disgustingly demanding. No. Things were quite all right as they were. She would not risk his displeasure. She would ask for nothing.

———

Donnigan lowered the pail into the deep well, his thoughts on Kathleen's response to the farm and house. Or rather her lack of it. He hadn't realized how important it had been to him that she would like what she found. Now he looked at his place through different eyes. What was wrong with it? Did she want a place like Erma's? Well, if she did, she had the wrong man. Lucas Stein was the only man in the whole territory who could afford a place like that.

He knew his place was—plain. But with a little effort and the few dollars he could give her, she could fix all that. Women knew how to go about such things. He didn't. Had he known, he would have done it for her—like planting the flowers.

And then he thought of the many changes and the long miles of travel. "She's just played out," he reasoned. "Give her a few days and she'll get things in shape the way she wants them."

Donnigan forced himself to whistle as he headed for the cabin with the fresh pail of well water in his hand.

Chapter Twelve

Settling In

The next morning dawned warm and bright, and Donnigan asked rather shyly if Kathleen would care to see the rest of the farm. She could hardly hide her enthusiasm but kept her face straight while she answered him that she would.

"Do you ride?" he surprised her.

She shook her head slowly.

"I have a mare that I've been working on for you," he went on, "but I don't think she's quite ready if you're not used to riding."

Kathleen wished to protest, but she bit her tongue.

"How do *you* check the farm?" she asked him.

"I ride Black," he answered.

"Black?"

"My stallion." He waited, watching her face, but she was giving him no hints whatever. "He rides double," he said at last.

Kathleen's head came up and for one unguarded moment her eyes flashed excitement.

"Would you mind?" asked Donnigan.

"No. No, I wouldn't mind," she said simply, hanging the dishcloth over the pan on the wall.

Kathleen may have become an expert at hiding her feelings, but even she slipped when she saw the black. He was magnificent. He was also a bit scary. *Could they both really ride him?* she wondered as the black horse raced around the corral, tossing his head and snorting.

At one whistle from Donnigan, the black dipped his head, snorted, and trotted obediently toward his owner. Kathleen longed to reach a hand out to the silky side of the animal, but she dared not do so without permission, and she refused to ask.

The black was soon bridled and saddled and Donnigan swung himself easily up. He reached down a hand for her. Black stomped impatiently, anxious to be off, but at a word from Donnigan he stopped his dancing.

"Give me your hand," said Donnigan. "Now, step up on my foot. When I lift, up you come behind me."

Kathleen reached up her hand, stepped on his foot and was lifted swiftly and easily from the ground to the back of the black horse. Never had she been up so high. It almost took her breath away.

"Put your arms around my waist and clasp your hands together," invited Donnigan.

Kathleen complied. She was glad that Donnigan could not see her flushed face.

"There's not much to see in the fields this time of year," Donnigan informed her. "The hay and crops are all in."

Donnigan held the black to a walk. The horse snorted his impatience and tossed his head, working the bit between his teeth. They traveled down a long lane, over the brow of a hill and past fields now empty of their summer's crops. The whole way the black sidestepped and danced and chomped at the bit.

"Does he always walk like this?" asked Kathleen innocently.

"He wants to run," said Donnigan.

Kathleen was silent for a few moments.

"Do you usually run?" she asked him.

"Usually," said Donnigan.

"Then—let him run," said Kathleen simply.

Donnigan half-turned in the saddle. "Are you sure?" he asked her. Kathleen nodded. Donnigan still looked doubtful.

"You'll have to hang on," he told her.

In answer she tightened her arms around him. He reached down with one hand to hold both of hers tightly and gave the black his head.

The horse answered immediately with a giant spring forward, and then they were rushing over the prairie grasses, the wind whipping at Kathleen's hair and fluttering her skirts. She had never experienced such an exhilarating sensation. On they went, covering the distance to the horse pasture in long strides, the muscles beneath her seeming to ripple with each forward lunge. Kathleen thought of the gentle roll of the sea.

They came to a fence and Donnigan pulled up the black with a soft "Whoa-a." Just on the other side of the fence a herd of horses was feeding. The black greeted them with an excited whinny, and many of the mares answered him. The herd began to stir, shifting, whirling, kicking up heels and playfully nipping one another.

The stallion stomped and pranced, eager to be back with his band.

"They're beautiful!" breathed Kathleen before she could check herself. "Whose are they?"

"Mine," replied Donnigan, pride coloring his voice. Then he blushed and corrected himself. "Ours." It was going to take some getting used to—this sharing of property, of their lives.

"Here, let me help you down," said Donnigan and reached his arm around to circle her waist. Kathleen felt herself being lifted up and out and lowered to the ground to stand beside the black. With one swift movement, Donnigan swung his leg over the black and joined her.

"We usually have to ride in to find them," Donnigan was explaining. "We were lucky today."

They stood for a moment watching the horses mill about. A few had approached the fence and extended their noses. The black moved eagerly forward to greet them. Others still ran and kicked and chased one another.

"Do they always act like that?" asked Kathleen.

"Only when the black comes around," replied Donnigan with a grin. "Then they show off a bit."

Kathleen would have liked to ask more questions but she held her tongue.

They watched the horses until the herd gradually settled. A few even went back to feeding.

"Ready?" asked Donnigan and Kathleen nodded. He gathered the reins and wheeled the reluctant stallion around, then mounted in one smooth motion and reached his hand for Kathleen. This time she did not need to be invited to place her arms around his waist. Firmly she clasped her hands together, hoping fervently that he would let the black run again. She could not hide her smile when he did. But Donnigan could not see it.

————

They surveyed the entire farm with its horses, cattle, fields, pastures, and woodlots before Donnigan turned the black toward home. They had been out for some hours. The day had grown hot, the hour past noon; still Kathleen was reluctant to relinquish the freedom she had felt when skimming across the prairie on the back of the big horse. She felt that she would just like to ride and ride—forever.

"I'll be in as soon as I take care of Black," Donnigan informed her as he eased her to the ground. Kathleen reached up a trembling hand to try to get her hair in order. The wind had wrenched the pins from their place.

She nodded her head slowly. She knew that Donnigan was saying that he would soon be in for his dinner.

Kathleen had never minded kitchen duties, so she washed her hands at the corner basin and began her search through the shelves. She found enough to fix them a proper dinner, but she realized that the American cupboard stock was different than what she had been used to.

Donnigan must have recognized the fact also, for as he washed at the basin later, he spoke without turning.

"We'll need to get into town soon and let you pick your

own fixin's. I haven't been in the habit of keeping much on hand."

Kathleen nodded, forgetting his back was to her.

He stood up straight to run the rough towel over his hands and face. "You can get the other things you'll want, too," he told her.

Her face must have registered her surprise. "What things?" she dared to ask.

"For the house. Whatever it is you need."

Kathleen let her gaze travel around the room. Oh, it was tempting. But she would not be demanding. Besides, Kathleen had never been given opportunity to "make a home" before. She didn't really know how one went about it—and she was afraid that she would make some terrible blunders if she attempted it. She did not want to risk the displeasure of the big man who stood opposite her in the cabin kitchen.

"The house is fine," she said, turning back to the stove. She missed seeing Donnigan's look of disappointment.

———

They were sitting on the porch enjoying the coolness of the fall evening. Kathleen had placed her shawl about her shoulders as the evenings could become chilly. They had shared this quiet time for almost four full weeks. It seemed a long time to Kathleen—and she still knew little more about Donnigan than she had the day she had entered his home. She longed to know—but remembered that he might resent her prodding. If there was one thing that Madam had stressed over and over, it was that a man didn't like being quizzed or nagged at.

Things had settled to a bit of a routine. Kathleen got the meals, did the laundry, kept the house clean. Donnigan cared for the animals, brought in the fresh pails of water and hauled the firewood. It seemed a good arrangement. In fact, Kathleen felt that she really should feel quite happy and contented. But she didn't. Deep down inside was a loneliness that hadn't been touched. In a way, she wondered if it really would have been that much different being a housemaid at Madam's new country home. She stole a glance at Donnigan, wondering if he could read her thoughts.

What bothered her the most was Donnigan's attitude. He still seemed to see her as a little girl. "Don't you lift that heavy pail." "Here, let me empty the wash water." "I'll build the fire." "I don't think the brown mare is ready for a young rider yet."

It galled Kathleen. She who had not just been independent but able to care for herself on the rough streets of London, and had also been responsible for others since she had been ten, was now being treated as if she were six.

At times it was all she could do to hold her temper in check. She was not a child. She was not without wits or ability. She was much stronger than he credited her with being. She was committed to this marriage—as strange as it was— but she longed to be an accepted partner, even if not an equal.

And she did long to ride the brown mare. The feeling that she had experienced on the black stallion with Donnigan holding the reins was only a taste of what it would be like to be in control of her own mount, she was sure. She couldn't wait to put her heels to the sides of the mare and sail over the brown hills and greened valleys.

———

Donnigan was sitting on the step whittling on a piece of wood. He couldn't have told why he had taken up whittling— except that it had helped to fill some of the lonely hours when he had been by himself in the house. He had rather hoped that he could put away his whittling knife with the coming of Kathleen. He knew that he would rather talk than whittle. But there didn't seem to be much talking done. He had looked forward to a winter of companionship—and here he was facing a winter of silence.

He had nothing against Kathleen—but she had not turned out to be what he had expected in a wife. He had wanted a woman who would come into his bare little cabin and fashion it into a home—warm and inviting and cozy. He had wanted a true companion—not just a maid in his kitchen. He had hoped for intimate chats about thoughts and feelings and dreams for the future. He had wanted someone to share every part of his life—and to let him be a part of hers. But Kathleen shut her thoughts and feelings away from him.

"It's her age," Donnigan told himself again. "When she matures—ages a bit—she'll open up more. I mustn't rush her. Give her time. Let her get the feeling that she belongs here."

Donnigan was pleased to see that the girl looked a bit healthier. She had been so pale, so weary, so frail, the first time he had set eyes on her. Already she seemed to be feeling much better, breathing in the fresh prairie air more deeply. Donnigan was glad for that. But he would be so glad when they were *really* partners. When Kathleen would look to him for companionship. For support. With all his heart he longed to give her more than a roof over her head, food at his table, the sharing of his bed at night.

His knife took a deeper cut than he had intended. His frustrations were showing in the work of his hands.

Donnigan hoped that his sigh did not reach the ears of Kathleen. Or if it did, that she wouldn't understand its meaning.

Kathleen sat on Erma's green and gold brocaded sofa and sipped tea. They had made it a habit to take tea together whenever Kathleen had a few extra minutes while in town.

"You are looking stronger, Kathleen—more—more robust," Erma observed.

Kathleen looked down at herself. Yes, she admitted, perhaps she was. Wasn't that one thing that had brought her to town? All her old dresses were getting too tight.

"I certainly feel better, I have to admit. I guess it's the fresh prairie air." She smiled at Erma.

"Or Donnigan," said Erma with a giggle.

Kathleen flushed. She had been Donnigan's wife for three months but she still blushed. For some strange reason she still felt like an imposter. A housekeeper.

"Do you ever get lonesome for home?" Erma surprised Kathleen by asking, and there was just the hint of sadness in her voice.

Kathleen thought about her answer. How much should she share? At last she nodded her head briefly. "Perhaps—just a bit—at times," she admitted, hoping that she wasn't giving anything away. Then she quickly added, "I guess that's natural enough."

"I guess," said Erma.

They both lifted their cups for another sip, then replaced them on the saucers.

"Do you?" asked Kathleen even though she felt she already knew the answer.

"A bit—at times," replied Erma.

Another sip of their tea.

"I suppose it's—it's because Lucas is so dreadfully busy," said Erma, then hastened as if to cover her confession. "I—mean—he is wonderful—just wonderful to me. I have everything—everything that I could possibly want. But he is so busy. He's such an important man. Why, he owns most of the town and he is so careful that everything be run—properly. I can't even imagine having so many things on my mind all at one time."

Kathleen nodded her head in support of Erma's claim. Everyone knew it for the truth.

"But he is so busy," Erma went on, her tone rather downcast. "He leaves long before I am up and doesn't come home some nights until I have fallen to sleep in my chair."

"What do you do with all your time?" asked Kathleen. Then quickly amended, "Not that you have spare time the way you keep things so spotlessly clean and—"

"Oh, I don't clean," explained Erma quickly. "The maid cleans—and the kitchen sends up our meals. If Lucas is too late, he sometimes stops at the dining room so he won't disturb me. He's very thoughtful, Lucas is." Erma gave Kathleen a forced smile.

"I would rather like to—to help out at the church or—or teach small children—or something—but Lucas says that wouldn't really be fitting," Erma went on thoughtfully.

She placed her cup and saucer on the delicate table by the sofa and smoothed imaginary wrinkles from her skirts. Then she looked up brightly. "Lucas says that my days will be more than full—once we have family," she said and color stained her cheeks.

"You are—are—?"

"I'm not sure—quite yet. But we do hope so. Lucas is so anxious for a son and I—well, I can hardly wait for a baby to—to help—" She stopped and toyed with the expensive looking rings on her fingers.

"I can hardly wait," she repeated with a little laugh, then rang for a maid to remove the tea things.

———

Donnigan hardly recognized Wallis when he met him on the street. The man was trimmed and pressed and polished until he shone.

"Well, aren't you looking fancy," Donnigan could not help but tease.

Wallis responded with a broad grin.

"And look at this," he invited showing his belt size. "I put on six pounds since she's been here."

"Must be a good cook," observed Donnigan. It was a known fact that Wallis hadn't been eating right for years.

"Good cook," said Wallis, nodding his head to emphasize the words. "Mighty good cook. Good at everything, that woman is. And can she work! Hey, I tell you that I never in my life seen anyone whip things into shape faster."

Donnigan reached out a hand and slapped his neighbor on the back. It was wonderful to see the man so happy.

"Haven't seen much of you lately," Donnigan observed. "Why don't you and Risa drop around for coffee?"

Wallis frowned slightly. "She ain't much for visitin'," he observed. "Oh, not thet she isn't friendly or all thet—it's just thet we got so much to do to catch up—to git the place in shape. We'll have time fer visitin' later on."

Donnigan nodded.

"You really outta stop by and see fer yerself how she's fixed up the place," said Wallis. "Ya wouldn't know it was the same cabin. Sure looks good. Sure does look good."

Again Donnigan nodded. He secretly wished that Kathleen had shown a bit more interest in fixing up their place; but if she was content with it as it was, why shouldn't he be?

A sharp whistle rent the air. Wallis spun on his heel and then turned back to Donnigan. "That's Risa. She's finished her shoppin'. She'll be wantin' to go." He turned, then said back over his shoulder, "That's the way she calls me." He grinned as though it was awfully cute to be summoned in such a way.

Chapter Thirteen

The Tempest

Kathleen lifted her head in surprise.

"I think I could put a lift on your shoe," Donnigan was saying.

The evenings were too cold now to sit out on the porch. Donnigan had brought his whittling indoors to the warm kitchen.

"A lift?" asked Kathleen.

"By building up the one shoe, the shorter leg would gain length. You wouldn't need to limp."

There, the truth was out. He was embarrassed about her limp.

"I worry about your spine," he went on simply. "I'm afraid the limp is hard on it."

Kathleen nodded mutely. Her back often ached so badly at night that she couldn't sleep. Could Donnigan be right?

"Do you mind if I try?" asked Donnigan.

Kathleen shook her head. She still wasn't sure if she should be thankful or offended.

Donnigan laid aside his whittling and crossed to where Kathleen sat near the stove.

"Let me see," said Donnigan. "Let me look at your boot."

Kathleen extended her legs, lifting her long skirts slightly as Donnigan knelt before her and carefully examined each foot.

"Now stand," said Donnigan. "Let's see how much—"

120

Kathleen obediently stood.

"Just as I thought," mused Donnigan as though to himself. "Not much at all—but it could make a real difference to your spine."

Donnigan worked many evenings before he was satisfied with the result. At last the boots were given to Kathleen for her to try.

At first the wooden lift made her foot feel clumsy and heavy, but Kathleen was surprised at how quickly she adjusted. Soon she was scurrying about the farm with scarcely a limp at all.

————

Kathleen stood at the kitchen window and stared balefully at the mounds of drifting snow. She had never heard such mournful wind, felt such bitter chill as with this early winter storm. Donnigan piled firewood almost to the ceiling of the cabin in his effort to keep her from shivering.

"You need warmer clothes," he told her, fussing over her again. "You're welcome to my flannel shirts, but I think you'd be swallowed up in them," he added, surveying her tiny form.

"As soon as the storm breaks, I'll head for town and look for some warm things for you," he told her. Kathleen shivered again, this time not just from the cold. Now he felt he had to dress her.

"At least put on a pair of my heavy wool socks," Donnigan invited as he stuffed more wood into the fire. "Helps a good deal if one's feet are warm."

Kathleen made a face behind his back, bit back her temper, and went to the bedroom to comply. She was committed to this marriage. She would not make a scene.

She hated to admit it, but the socks did help considerably. She even managed to stop her shivering.

What made her the most angry about the storm was that she was cooped up indoors after finally being given Donnigan's permission to ride. After many hours of gentling the brown mare, he had decided that she was ready for Kathleen—within reason. Kathleen was not to ride alone, not to ride the canyon trails south of the pasture, not to allow the mare her head. Kathleen inwardly chaffed over all the restrictions, but she did not argue. She did not wish the privilege to be retracted.

"I thought you might like to name her," Donnigan had said as he presented the reins to Kathleen for the first time.

"You haven't named her yet?" Kathleen asked in surprise.

Donnigan nodded. "I did," he replied, "but my names are never too fancy."

Kathleen had thought of the big black stallion. She certainly would have named him something different than Black had she been doing the choosing, so she nodded in silent agreement.

Kathleen ran her hand over the smooth nose of the mare and along the shiny neck. "Make friends with her," Donnigan advised, "but let her know who's boss."

It wouldn't be hard for Kathleen to make friends. She already loved the mare.

Kathleen had named her new mount Shee. "It means elf. My father used to tell me stories about them," she explained to Donnigan. If he had thought it a strange name for a horse, he had not said so.

They had gone for one ride. The day had been sunny but brisk. They both knew that winter was already rapping gently on Nature's door and would soon make entrance into their world. Kathleen longed to hold it back. She hated the thought of being confined to the cabin at the very time she had been given access to the trails of Donnigan's farmlands.

One ride together—one glorious ride, and then the storm had come and shut her in.

Kathleen turned her back to the window and winter. She didn't want to acknowledge the storm. Because of it she was stuck in the cabin being Donnigan's little girl again. She had hoped that the freedom she felt on the horse's back would help her to feel more like an adult, would help Donnigan see her as an adult.

———

When the storm's fury had broken, Donnigan went to town. It was still too cold for Kathleen to endure a trip on the cold wagon seat, he told her. Once she had warmer clothes they would go to town together.

In her agitation, Kathleen paced the kitchen, stopping occasionally to shove split logs into the fire with more force than necessary. It was a long day. She thought about going to the barn and saddling Shee for a ride but decided it would be better not to. Donnigan had handled the saddling chores. Kathleen wasn't quite sure if she could do it right.

"I need to watch what he does so I can do it for myself," she determined and paced the floor some more.

"I can at least go to the barn," she finally decided. The horses seemed pleased to see her. She stroked the brown neck of Shee and tried the curry a bit. She even dared to lean across the manger and rub the black's nose. He snorted and jerked his head, and Kathleen jumped back so quickly that she bumped her head on a support pole.

She decided to give the horses a treat of oats. Just then she heard the rumble of the wagon in the yard. Donnigan was home. She supposed that she should be excited about new clothes. At least curious about what a man would pick. But Kathleen was not. She would have preferred to do her own choosing.

So Kathleen deliberately stalled, slowly scooping oats from the sack nearby and dumping them in the manger bin. The horses snorted and plunged in their noses. Kathleen smiled to herself. She added scoop after scoop until the bins were full. When she could fit no more to the generous helping, she idly tossed the scoop back toward the sack and took her time leaving the barn.

Donnigan was just coming toward her with the team.

"Howdy," he called in good nature, then frowned slightly. "You better get in," he added. "You'll be catching your death of cold."

Kathleen wrinkled her nose but headed for the house.

Donnigan did not join her for some time. Kathleen put the coffeepot on. He would be chilled and would appreciate a cup.

She stoked the fire again so that the pot would boil quickly.

When Donnigan pushed his way through the door, his arms were filled with packages.

Looks like he bought out the store, Kathleen thought to herself, and in spite of her resolve she felt a stirring of interest.

But Donnigan looked bothered by something. Never had she seen such darkness in his eyes.

She wished to ask what was wrong, but she bit back the question. It was none of her business, was it?

Donnigan deposited all the parcels on the table. They filled the whole area. Kathleen wondered where he expected her to serve the coffee.

"Should I take—these—to the bedroom?" she asked when he turned to remove his heavy jacket and hang it on the peg by the door.

"Do whatever you want with them," Donnigan replied in a tone she had not heard him use before. "They're yours."

Kathleen's eyes widened. Something was wrong and that was for sure.

He washed his hands at the basin. She waited for the explosion she was sure would occur. She had remembered hearing that tone in her father's voice, and it had always been followed by a display of his Irish temper.

"Kathleen," Donnigan said as he reached for the towel. His voice was controlled—too controlled, as though fighting for patience with an erring child. "Don't ever feed the horses."

Kathleen stared at him in surprise. Surely—surely that wasn't a sin. Was he so possessive—?

"It could have killed them." His words were almost sharp. Blunt and stabbing.

Kathleen gasped and groped for some response. "I—I only gave them oats," she managed to say.

He just nodded.

"I've seen you give them oats." Kathleen was surprised at her own boldness. She who had determined not to cause any friction in this marriage was actually answering back to her husband. Madam would have been shocked.

"Yes," he said and returned the towel to the peg with one quick jerk. She felt that he was losing a bit of his control as well. "Very carefully measured oats," he said, his face taut with emotion. "If I hadn't happened home when I did—if those two horses had eaten what they had been given—" He stopped, seemingly unable to even think of the consequences.

He ran a trembling hand through his hair. She waited—her own hand fumbling with the parcel nearest her.

He took a deep breath, fighting hard to get himself in control again. When he spoke, his voice was low and almost pleading. As if he were talking to a child, Kathleen thought, and anger filled her whole being.

"Kathleen." He crossed the kitchen and stood close to her. "I know the farm is new to you. I know that you have never learned to—to care for stock and—and such. But please—don't—don't do things without checking with me. Oats—too many oats—can founder horses. Can kill them at times. We could have lost both horses. The mare and—and Black." He was almost white with the enormity of her misdeed.

Kathleen's own face went pale. She had not known. How could she have known?

"Sure then, and why didn't you tell me?" she demanded. "Why don't you teach me? You won't even talk to me other than telling me what I should or should not do." Her voice rose as she spoke until she found herself shouting. "You just—just keep treating me like—like I am a child. I'm not! I'm almost eighteen. And I'm not stupid either. I can learn. I'm an adult. Not a child who needs your coddling. Treat me like an adult. Give me some respect." And with the last words Kathleen's hand sought the nearest parcel of yardgoods and hurled it at Donnigan. She did not wait for his response. With sobs of anguish she ran to the little bedroom and slammed the door with such force the whole cabin trembled.

She flung herself on the bed and cried. Cried for home and Bridget. Cried for her missing father. Cried because of the empty, lonely place in her heart that would not go away. And cried for her marriage—the one she had just managed to destroy with her outburst. Surely Donnigan would never be able to forgive her for the way she had acted and the angry words she had hurled at him along with the wrapped material. She had just proved that she was indeed the child he thought her to be.

———————

Donnigan lowered himself slowly to a kitchen chair and put his head in his hand. He had really done it. He had told himself all the way from the barn to the house that he must keep his control. That Kathleen did not know better. That he must not let his fright show as he spoke to her. But he had messed up the whole thing. Had really messed up. He wondered if he could ever make things right.

No, no, he guessed he couldn't. Things had never been right, not from the very beginning. This whole thing—this whole arranged marriage was a sham and a shame right from the start. He had been a fool. A blind fool to let Wallis and Lucas talk him into such a scheme.

But hadn't he become involved of his own free will? Wasn't it his decision? No one had twisted his arm that he had remembered. He couldn't go laying the blame at his neighbors' doors.

Donnigan lifted his head and ran his hand nervously through his hair. No. It was his fault. He had to take the full blame. He just hadn't been ready for marriage. Oh, he thought he was. Longed for a wife and even children. But Kathleen was so—so young and so—so— That was the trouble. He had ordered a wife and they had sent him a child.

Though he never would have dared to share his feelings with Kathleen, daily he worried that she might announce she was expecting a child herself. His child. She was too young, too frail to bear his baby. It was a fear that haunted him—that sometimes kept him awake in the darkness as he felt the strands of her dark hair touch his shoulder and listened to her even breathing as she slept.

And now—now he had hurt her deeply. So deeply that he had no idea of how to go about repairing the damage. Were they to go on and on in this marriage, shut away from each other? He didn't know if he could stand it.

He shook himself free from his dark thoughts and rose to get a cup of the boiling coffee.

He had no choice. He was in the marriage now. Whether it was a good one—or a poor one—had little bearing. Kathleen was his responsibility. He would care for her in the best way he knew how.

Kathleen cried until she was exhausted. At last she fell into a troubled sleep. When she at last awoke, the bedroom window told her that darkness had fallen. Unconsciously she shifted on the bed, trying to sense if Donnigan slept beside her.

She felt a pang of concern when she discovered his absence, and then another pang when she remembered what had brought her to the room in the first place.

"He will be so angry with me," she mourned and rolled back over to bury her head in the pillow for a fresh burst of tears.

"What do I do now? Oh, what do I do?"

In spite of her desire to stay right where she was with her sorrow, she forced herself to stir.

"It's past supper," she scolded herself, not one to avoid responsibility. "He'll be hungry."

Kathleen reached up to calm her tumbling hair. The pins had come loose as she had tossed in her sleep. She didn't wish to take the time to repin it, so she lifted the comb and ran it quickly through the dark, tangled curls, letting them tumble about her shoulders in girlish fashion.

"Now he will really think me a child," she said to herself, and anger burned her cheeks again.

He was sitting silently in his big chair when she quietly

slipped out to the kitchen. A newspaper was spread across his knees, but she noticed that his eyes were not upon it. At the sound of her entrance he roused and looked at her.

"Did you sleep well?" The words sounded choked. Forced. She heard him swallow.

"Well enough," she managed to respond and moved to the stove. She noticed that the parcels had all been removed from the table and were carefully stacked in a corner.

"I've eaten," he said woodenly. "There's enough in the pot for your supper."

Kathleen didn't feel like eating. She moved the pot from the back of the stove where it had been keeping warm and turned to the small cupboard. She would just do the cleaning up and then go back to bed.

But the cleaning up had also been done. The dishes were all neatly stacked back on the shelves.

The wind howled outside again, rattling the branch that always scratched against the house. Kathleen shuddered.

"Another storm moving in," observed Donnigan. "Good thing I managed to get to town for—" Then he stopped short.

He changed the topic quickly, rising from his chair and heading for his heavy coat. "Erma sent you a note," he said. "I had her help me with the—the choosing."

Kathleen's full attention was immediate. She accepted the note and pulled a chair up close to the table and the lamp and began to read the short letter.

Dear Kathleen,

I have just been dying to see you. I do hope that the weather will soon improve so you can come to town. I have so much to talk to you about.

We are going to have a baby! Lucas is so excited. He has already picked the name for his son. I can hardly wait. I've started my sewing. Lucas says at the rate that I am going, it will have to be triplets to make use of all the things.

Come and see me as soon as you can.

With warmest regards,

Erma

Kathleen carefully folded the letter and placed it in her apron pocket. How she envied Erma. Erma who was expecting a child. Erma who Lucas allowed to be a woman. Erma who now shared with a man the most intimate experience a woman could ever share—the plans and dreams and preparations of the coming of a child to their home. Kathleen felt like crying again. She dared not look toward Donnigan.

She rose from her chair and retreated to the bedroom. She was still awake when, much later, Donnigan joined her. She turned her back and feigned sleep. She wasn't sure she liked the man. She might even hate him.

Chapter Fourteen

A Long Talk

Nothing further was said about the incident. They seemed to declare an unspoken truce. Kathleen was not sure if she was sorry or relieved. After a few days of strained silence, life went on much as it had before.

Kathleen did not go near the barn again, though she longed to pay a visit to Shee. Instead, she spent her time with needle in hand, sewing up garments from the material Donnigan had purchased. She would not have let herself express her joy at having new clothes of her very own, clothes that would actually fit properly, but she felt thankfulness nonetheless. She was quite willing, in her thinking, to lay all the credit at Erma's door.

———

Donnigan was glad for winter chores. As every winter, the horses and cattle had been moved to the pasture adjoining the corrals so that they could be more easily cared for. The saddle horses and team were kept in the barn except on the warmer days. That meant barn cleaning, a job that Donnigan had once deplored. Now he welcomed even that, for it took him from the close confines of the kitchen. He took to talking to the black again. At first he felt awkward and embarrassed, but when the black rubbed his nose on the man's sleeve as though he had been missing the conversations,

Donnigan waved aside his feelings and enjoyed his little one-sided chats.

He did not discuss Kathleen—or his empty marriage. That was far too personal even to share with a horse. Instead, he talked about the weather, the other farm animals, or his plans for spring.

At times Donnigan found himself envying Lucas. The man seemed totally pleased with his marriage. He always spoke about how he was teaching Erma this or telling her about that. It seemed to Donnigan that the two really talked.

Donnigan missed Wallis. He would have loved to slip over to the neighbor's farm for a manly chat and a cup of the bitter coffee. But Wallis gave all indications of being more than wrapped up in his new wife. Folks joked in town about Wallis becoming henpecked. She whistled—he ran. But if Wallis didn't mind the arrangement, why should anyone else fuss, Donnigan reasoned.

No, it seemed that he was really the only one of the three who had struck out. And he couldn't blame it on the young Kathleen. He had been surprised to hear her declare that she was seventeen. Though still young, she was older than he had thought. He had feared that she might be closer to fifteen. Almost eighteen, she had said. Donnigan had known many girls who were married by eighteen. It was Kathleen's size that had fooled him. She was so tiny. So frail.

No, actually she wasn't that frail anymore. Oh, she was still a small, dainty woman, but she wasn't frail. She looked much better than when she had first arrived. And she was much stronger than she looked, he granted her that.

She had said that he treated her like a child, and with a flush to his cheeks, he admitted that he had. He had such a time thinking of her as anything else. But he was working on it. He really was.

———

They were invited to share Christmas with Lucas and Erma. Kathleen was sure that Lucas's invitation had come in response to Erma's pleading. But she was just thankful for the opportunity to get out of the house for a day.

The weather cooperated. It was still cold, but the wind was not blowing, and the sun was weakly sharing its rays with the world. Kathleen wore her favorite of the new garments and wrapped her warmest shawl closely about her shoulders. She saw Donnigan toss a couple of warm blankets in the sled, but he refrained from telling her that she should wrap up in them.

Erma was still not "showing"—except in her face that seemed to glow. Again Kathleen felt envy wash over her. Erma had so much.

Lucas, always the good host, had arranged a complete turkey dinner for them to eat in the hotel dining room rather than up in the suite. "Food odors sometimes bother Erma," Lucas explained.

But Kathleen cared not where she was served. It was so good to get out. So nice to be with other people.

After the dinner, Lucas needed his cigar, so he and Donnigan stayed to chat in the dining room while Erma and Kathleen went to the rooms above.

"I can hardly wait to show you all the baby things," Erma enthused as they climbed the stairs.

Lucas had been right. Erma had already filled a chest with carefully stitched little garments. Kathleen wondered how she would fill her next six months.

"You are really happy, aren't you, Erma?" Kathleen could not help but say.

"Oh yes!" exclaimed the young woman. "It has made so much difference to be—to be waiting for a child. My hours have meaning now. The days aren't nearly so lonely. And Lucas—Lucas comes home every morning, promptly at ten, so that I can get some fresh air and some exercise."

At Kathleen's puzzled look, Erma hurried to explain.

"It isn't proper for a woman to be out on the streets alone," she said, "so Lucas comes home and takes me for a walk."

Kathleen could only stare. Poor Erma had been virtually a prisoner in her own suite of rooms.

"When I get too—too—obvious to be on the streets of town, Lucas says that we will drive to the country, tie the carriage, and go for a little walk down some private trail."

Kathleen's mouth fell open. She quickly put aside her envy. At least Donnigan allowed her *some* freedom.

"Oh, Lucas has been reading up on it," Erma hurried on, not understanding Kathleen's expression. "One must have fresh air and exercise—for the sake of the mother and the baby."

————

For all Donnigan's fretting about her coming down with a cold, it was he himself who came in from chores with a flushed face and a sore throat.

Kathleen racked her brain for a home remedy that would keep the man on his feet, but came up empty.

The next morning he was dreadfully fevered. When he forced himself from the bed and tried to pull on his flannel shirt, Kathleen saw him shaking.

"What's wrong?" she asked, fear in her voice.

"I'm all right," he insisted.

"You're not all right," Kathleen flung back at him. "You're shaking all over."

"Just the chills," he responded. "I'll be fine."

Kathleen threw back the warm blankets and bounded to her feet.

"You won't be fine. Look at you."

She crossed to him and reached her hand up to his forehead. "Sure, and you're burning with fever!" she exclaimed, fear gripping her.

She pushed her feet into knitted house slippers to ward off the chill of the wooden floor.

"You'd best get back to bed," she instructed. "I'll see to the fire."

"I can't," argued Donnigan. "I've got to care for the stock."

"I'll care for the stock," responded Kathleen, already reaching for her warmest skirt.

"But you can't—" began Donnigan.

"I can—and I will," said Kathleen with boldness, the determination in her voice unmistakable. "That is—if you'll be good enough to tell me what to do."

Donnigan did not miss the challenge. He stared at Kathleen for a moment, seeing the dark flashing of her eyes.

He removed the shirt from his shoulders and tossed it on the floor by the bed.

"I'll tell you," he said meekly and climbed back under the covers.

Carefully and fully Donnigan explained the chore procedures to Kathleen. From time to time she nodded her head as an indication that she had understood. By the time he had finished his explanation, he was drenched in a cold sweat. Even he had to admit that he would not have been able to get up.

"If you need help, go for Wallis," he managed before lapsing into a fit of coughing.

"I won't need help," said Kathleen firmly. "I'll bring you something for your throat—then you stay put."

———

Donnigan was dreadfully ill, and Kathleen was dreadfully worried. She had none of the things that had been used in her London home to fight colds and influenza. She really didn't know what to do for Donnigan except to try to relieve his mind concerning the stock and to sponge bathe him to bring down his fever. She offered him soup and tea as often as she could coax him into taking a few swallows, but found it difficult to get him to try food.

It was almost two weeks before Donnigan felt strong enough to stir around the kitchen. Kathleen had put in many, many long hard days. The weather had not been kind. She had needed to fight the elements as well as his illness. And the chores had taken much of her strength and time. There had even been a cow who had calved out of season. Kathleen had put her in the barn, managed to quiet her, and promptly informed her that she would from henceforth be responsible to provide them with milk.

"She's never been milked," argued Donnigan when Kathleen told him that she had herself a milk cow.

"She has now," announced Kathleen and thrust a custard pudding in his hand.

"But how did you—?" began Donnigan.

"I bribed her with chop—and tied her legs," replied Kathleen simply.

"What about the calf?" asked Donnigan.

"The calf is drinking fine from a pail. There's plenty for all of us."

Donnigan could only shake his head and smile.

At last Donnigan was strong enough to return to the chores. Kathleen did not argue but inwardly she knew that she would miss the choring. She wouldn't deny that it had been difficult work. But it was a nice change to get out of the house. And she enjoyed working with the animals. She even chatted as she curried the horses or milked the now-cooperative cow. She did not look forward to being shut up in the kitchen again. In spite of the additional work, Kathleen concluded that she had never in her life really felt so good.

Much of it was due, she was sure, to the lift on the shoe. It did help her whole body to have her spine kept straight as she moved about. And when each of those long hard days came to an end, she slept as never before.

"We need to talk," said Donnigan, pushing back his empty supper plate.

Kathleen's head came up. Donnigan had now returned to his chores. Had he discovered something she had left undone? Or not done right? She found her mind scrambling to try to sort out where she might have failed.

"I did a lot of thinking while I lay there in bed," said Donnigan.

Kathleen still stared, not sure where he was headed.

"You said I think of you as a child," said Donnigan, and Kathleen drew in her breath. So, after all the weeks that had passed, they were finally going to go back to their quarrel. It appeared that Donnigan had a long memory. Kathleen had hoped that they could forget what had been said that evening. Now it seemed that Donnigan was going to open old wounds. Kathleen turned to face him, her chin lifting.

"I think of you as a child," he repeated. "How?"

It was the wrong question. Kathleen felt the color rush to her cheeks. She lifted eyes filled with hurt and defiance. She was right back to where she was when she had flung the parcel at him and headed for the bedroom.

"How?" she spat at him. "How? In every way, that's how."

Donnigan cursed under his breath. He was going at all this the wrong way again.

"You—you—" Kathleen was suddenly so angry again that she could not find the words to accuse him.

Donnigan reached out to touch her arm, and she flung his hand off as she faced him.

"I'm only asking so I can find out what I need to correct," he said quickly, but there was a bit of bite to his words as well.

Kathleen just stared.

Donnigan rose to his feet and began to pace the room. He rubbed his hands together in front of him as though deeply seeking answers—direction.

"I don't know about you," he said at last, still pacing, "but I'm not exactly happy with this marriage, and I might as well say it."

Kathleen sucked in her breath again. She felt that she had been slapped. She had tried so hard not to make fusses. Not to demand and now—

"And I'm not putting the blame on you," Donnigan hurried to explain. "Truth is"—he stopped pacing and faced her—"I haven't known how to be a husband."

His honest and frank confession caught her totally off guard. She had expected him to point the finger at her. Instead, he stood before her with a look of shame and embarrassment.

"I need your help, Kathleen." There was pleading in his voice.

She lowered her head so she wouldn't have to see the pain in his eyes.

"You were right," he confessed further, resuming his pacing again. "I—did think of you as a child. I still—still fight it. But I know—I've seen—that you are a woman. A woman that I would like to share my life with—but I need help."

All of the anger drained from Kathleen. She sat motionless except for the trembling of her shoulders.

"What's wrong with us, Kathleen?" he begged. "What are we doing wrong? Why aren't we happy—instead of—of just living together?"

Kathleen sat for one moment, observing the bent shoulders of the strong young man before her. She had been braced for a fight. She could not fight this.

"I don't know," she whispered, her defenses crumbling. All her loneliness and longing tumbled in upon her. Her hands came up to cover her face, and the tears dripped between her fingers.

In two quick strides he was there, gathering her into his arms, holding her close against his chest, pressing kisses against her hair.

"Oh, Kathleen," she heard him murmur over and over. "Kathleen, I do love you. I really do. Help me to show you. Please, Kathleen."

She cried against him until she had no more tears. He brushed them away with his fingers and wiped them on his shirt sleeve. When she was finally able to look up at him, she noticed tearstains on his cheeks as well.

"We'll make it," he whispered. "We'll make it—but I want us to be happy. Both of us."

He pulled her even closer and kissed her again.

"So what do we do?" asked Kathleen with a trembling

voice as soon as she was able to speak.

He shook his head. "I don't know," he answered truthfully. "I don't have the answers—but I think we need to talk."

Talk. Oh, how Kathleen longed to talk. To really talk. Not just to say, "Good morning. Did you sleep well? Please pass the biscuits." No, really talk.

She nodded and wiped her nose on a handkerchief from her apron pocket.

"Where do we start?" she managed.

"I don't know." Slowly he released her. "There is so much that we still haven't said. So much we haven't shared." Then he dared to go on. "I have longed to talk, but I thought you— you weren't ready to share your past—your heart. I was waiting—"

"And I wanted to talk," Kathleen laughed shakily, "but Madam always said a man didn't want a—a chatterer."

"Chatterer? That was one reason I sent for a wife—so I wouldn't have to talk to Black."

Kathleen laughed again. So he talked to the animals, too. It seemed funny. Ironical.

He sat down on a kitchen chair and pulled her onto his knees. "Let's talk," he said with a grin. "Let's talk all night if we want to. Let the dishes wait. I want to know all about you. I want you to know all about me."

Kathleen put her arms around his neck and drew his head against her. It was almost surprising for her to discover that she didn't hate him after all. She had never felt such deep, fervent love.

Chapter Fifteen

Erma

Once the door had been opened to real communication, Kathleen felt that she could not get enough. At times she wondered if she really was becoming a chattering woman, but Donnigan seemed to enjoy it. He nodded and smiled and made comments of his own, and night after night, before they knew it, the evening was gone and it was time to retire again.

"How much more quickly time goes when you have someone to talk to," Kathleen mused.

"Is Black missing your conversations?" she teased Donnigan one evening as they sat by the fire, she with a sock to darn and he with one of his old newspapers.

He grinned. "I talk to him now and then just so he won't feel left out," he teased back.

Kathleen chuckled. "And I still talk to Polly when I milk her," she admitted.

Kathleen had insisted that she be the one to milk the cow morning and night. It was good to get out of the kitchen and breathe a breath of fresh air. And Polly was milked in the barn, so it was never too cold.

They were silent while Kathleen threaded her needle. But the silence was no longer cold and threatening. They both knew they could break it if they had an idea they wished to discuss, a thought to share, or just an event of the day to tell about.

Donnigan's eyes went back to his paper.

"What are you?" Kathleen asked suddenly, causing Donnigan's head to lift.

"What am I?" He hesitated. "A man—I hope."

Kathleen chuckled. "I mean—what nationality? What were your kin?"

Donnigan shrugged carelessly. "I dunno."

"Donnigan *sounds* Irish," Kathleen commented.

"You know an Irishman named Donnigan?"

Kathleen made another stitch. "No," she admitted. "But when I first saw your name on that piece of paper, I thought maybe it was Irish."

"Well, I've never met another man—or boy—in my whole life who answered to the name," said Donnigan, his tone ironic.

"I wonder what nationality it is. Where it came from," Kathleen said as she placed another stitch.

Donnigan shrugged again.

"Don't you care?" asked Kathleen. "I mean, I'm an O'Malley. I've been told that all my life. My father made me feel proud to be Irish. And you don't even know what you are. Doesn't it matter at all to you?"

"Guess not. I've never given it much thought. What difference does it make? Men are—men. People are people. No difference."

Kathleen glanced up at him, surprised by his attitude.

"But wouldn't you like to know if you are French or German or British—or Irish?" she asked in mock exasperation.

"Don't think I'm Irish," Donnigan returned.

"Sure now, and you definitely are not," said Kathleen pertly, her accent strengthening for the first time in a long while. "An Irishman knows what he is, and that's the pure truth of it."

Donnigan smiled.

"Sure now," he tried to mimic her.

Kathleen threw the newly darned sock at him and he rose quickly from his chair, chasing her around the kitchen and stuffing the mended sock down the front of her gown.

"You can never be serious," she accused him, though she knew it wasn't true.

"I'm serious," he answered, but his voice still held teasing.

"Then tell me where you ever got a name like Donnigan."

He still held her around the waist. "I don't know," he replied. "My mother named me, I was told. Where she got it—or why she liked it—I'll never know."

"Don't you like it?"

He released her then. "If you had any idea how many fights I had as a youngster over this name of mine—"

"But why?"

"I've no idea. It's just—just different."

"Then why haven't you changed it? You could go by Don or—or—"

"Guess that's the reason I fought. Fellas were always trying to call me something else. Pin a nickname on me. And I kept insisting that my name was Donnigan—and that they call me that."

In their short time together Kathleen had heard Donnigan correct a storekeeper who didn't call him by his full name. He had not been rude. Just simply stated, "The name is Donnigan." At the time she had been surprised that he would make an issue of it. She was especially surprised now when he confessed he didn't even like the name.

But Donnigan had become serious. "I lost my mother when I was very young," he said with deep feeling. "My name is the one thing I have from her. Guess that seemed reason enough to fight for it."

Seeing the pain in his eyes, Kathleen wished she hadn't asked.

———

A rider pounded into the farmyard, a young boy from town. Kathleen and Donnigan were both surprised. Rarely did they have company and never anyone who came so obviously on a mission. Donnigan met him at the door.

"Is Mrs. Harrison in?" he asked, sounding out of breath.

Kathleen moved to the door, her eyes wide with concern. The young lad reached up to remove his cap.

"I've a note for you, ma'am—from Mr. Stein," the boy said, and handed Kathleen an envelope.

Kathleen's hand began to tremble. *Whatever would Lucas have to say to her that would require courier service—and at such speed,* she wondered.

By the time she had crossed to a kitchen chair and torn open the envelope, Donnigan was shutting the door. The boy was gone.

Donnigan came to stand beside her and she held the note so he could read over her shoulder.

"Dear Mrs. Harrison," the note began.

"Please excuse my liberty in calling on you, but Erma is asking for you to come. She fears she is losing the baby.

"Lucas Stein."

"Oh no," sobbed Kathleen, her eyes wide with the tragedy of it.

"I'll get the team."

"Wouldn't it be faster to ride?" asked Kathleen, already going toward the bedroom to change into warmer clothing.

He hesitated for only a moment, then nodded. "I'll get the horses," he said and reached for his Stetson.

Kathleen quickly changed her dress for one more appropriate for riding. She pinned her hair tightly and secured her bonnet. Then she reached for a warm sweater. A shawl simply would not do for riding Shee at a gallop.

Even as she hurried, her mind was in a spin. Erma might lose her baby. She would be crushed. But what could she, Kathleen, do about it? She was not a doctor. Kathleen inwardly pleaded with a God she hoped might listen that the baby and Erma would be okay.

By the time Kathleen closed the door behind her, Donnigan was bringing the horses toward the house. He helped Kathleen up into her saddle and then mounted Black. Both horses had been lacking in exercise and wanted to run.

"Hold her in check," Donnigan couldn't help but caution.

"She hasn't been ridden for a while."

Kathleen nodded. But it was hard. Not only did the mare wish to run, but Kathleen wished that she could let her. It was Donnigan who kept them under control.

By the time they reached the hotel it was all over. Erma had lost the baby. Kathleen found her sobbing uncontrollably. Lucas paced the floor beside the bed. Truly this was one event totally out of his control.

A doctor had been called from Raeford, but he had not arrived until it was too late. He did give Erma something to make her sleep and gently eased Kathleen from the room as soon as Erma's eyes became heavy.

"She needs her rest," he whispered. "That is all that we can do for her now."

Kathleen felt sick inside. It was so hard for Erma to lose the child—to pack away all her hopes and dreams along with the little garments in the chest at the end of the bed.

Kathleen longed to reach out with help for her friend. What could she say? What could she do? The ride back home was a silent one.

Kathleen went to see Erma often over the next weeks. Donnigan felt more and more confident with her handling of the mare and even got so he let her go alone. He may not have been quite so at ease had he known that once out of sight of the house, Kathleen often gave the mare her head. She loved the feel of the wind as it tugged at her bonnet and whipped her skirts.

Nor would he have felt at ease had Kathleen confessed that she thought—she just thought there might be a chance that she too was expecting a child.

But Donnigan knew nothing about either, and so Kathleen rode to town alone and rode at her own pace.

Each time she entered the suite of hotel rooms, she hoped with all her heart that she would find some improvement in Erma's state of mind. But always she was disappointed.

"I don't know what I did wrong. I don't know," Erma wailed again and again.

"Sure now, and you didn't do anything wrong," Kathleen tried to comfort her. "Sometimes those things just happen."

"But Lucas read all the books. We did all the things they said."

Kathleen felt impatient with Lucas and his books. It was all she could do to keep from telling Erma so.

"Lucas is so upset with me," went on Erma. "He thinks I must have done something—something to hurt the baby."

"Such nonsense!" Kathleen fairly exploded.

"Oh—I wanted that baby so much," moaned Erma. "So much."

Kathleen longed to tell her, "There will be other babies," but she didn't dare speak the words.

———

"How is she?" Donnigan asked, meeting Kathleen in the farmyard after a visit to Erma.

"Not good," she replied, frustration in her voice. "She just continues to grieve and grieve."

"I guess that's understandable," said Donnigan, taking the mare's rein and helping Kathleen dismount. "She was so looking forward to having the child."

"But she must stop her moaning," said Kathleen. "After all, she can have another child. There is nothing physically wrong with her, Dr. Heggith says. She just has to get ahold of herself."

Donnigan looked a bit surprised at Kathleen's outburst. He turned the mare toward the barn. "Maybe she will—soon," he said.

They walked a few paces before Donnigan broke the silence.

"Do you think it's that easy?" he asked.

"Of course I don't think it's easy," responded Kathleen in a quieter tone. "Of course not—easy—but necessary. One has to go on with life no matter how one feels. I know how she must be feeling. If I lost my baby—"

Donnigan stopped short.

"If you what?" he asked abruptly.

Kathleen flushed. She still hadn't told him, but she was quite sure now. She had been waiting for just the right time. She took a deep breath, then another step toward the barn.

But Donnigan's hand on her shoulder stopped her.

"What are you saying?" he asked her bluntly.

Kathleen stopped, looked at him with a flushed face, and lowered her head.

"I thought we made a promise—that we would talk to each other—tell each other everything," Donnigan said, hurt and distance in his voice.

"I was going to tell you," defended Kathleen.

"Then it's true?"

Kathleen nodded her head.

She hated the pained look in Donnigan's eyes. He looked directly at her for what seemed a terrible length of time; then he moved away to lead the mare into the barn.

Kathleen watched him go, shifting uncomfortably from one foot to the other, then turned and went to the house.

———

"Donnigan—I'm sorry," Kathleen whispered into the darkness after they had retired.

He had brushed a kiss against her cheek, said good-night in a strained manner, then turned on his side, his back to her.

Kathleen feared he might be angry that they were going to have a child. If that was so—she would also be angry right back at him. Didn't children go with marriage?

She gathered her courage and decided to try again. As Donnigan had reminded her, they had promised to talk things out.

"Don't you want to be a father?" she asked his back.

"Of course I do," he responded immediately.

"Then why—"

"I think I had a right to know—without it being a—a blunder," he said.

She knew then that she had hurt him deeply.

"I was going to tell you—soon," she defended. "It's just—just I've been so worried about Erma."

"What about my worry?" asked Donnigan, still not turning to her.

"Your worry?" she said, puzzled.

He half-turned. "About you—about our baby," he answered with a trembling voice.

"What do you mean? I'm fine. The baby is—is just beginning."

"I'm worried about you, Kathleen. You said I saw you as a child. Well, I've changed that. I'm—I'm trying hard to change that. But even if you are a—a woman, you are still—still small. Maybe too small to—to have a child."

Kathleen lay beside him, listening to his words. She began to understand his fears.

"I'm the same size as my mother was—and she had me," she informed him gently. "And her mother was even smaller, so she told me, and she had seven babies, and that's the pure truth of it."

"Oh, Kathleen," moaned Donnigan, and he turned over to gather her close. "If anything should happen—"

"It won't," she tried to assure him. "It won't."

———

Kathleen still went to see Erma as often as she could, but Donnigan now insisted upon driving her to town—slowly. The trips wasted a whole day and Kathleen chaffed with each step that the plodding team made. But she dared not argue. She could still read concern in Donnigan's eyes each time they talked of the baby. She wanted to give him all the reason for assurance that she could.

Erma did not show any sign of improving. She was out of bed now, but she still spent her days grieving and sorrowing over what should have been the happiest summer of her life. Kathleen sensed that the loss of the baby was putting a terrible strain on Erma's marriage. She fervently wished she could do *something* for her friend.

Chapter Sixteen

Sean

When spring finally came, Donnigan was so busy in the fields that Kathleen felt she hardly saw him. She missed him around the kitchen. But she understood about the planting of the crops.

Often on warm days she packed a lunch, filled a pail with cool well water, and walked to the fields to picnic with him while the horses munched on nearby grasses. Those were good times for Kathleen and she felt that Donnigan looked forward to her noon visits.

He had built the chicken pen as promised, and it was now filled with half a dozen hens and a cocky rooster. Kathleen hoped to increase the flock, so she set aside eggs while she waited for some of the hens to decide to brood.

She had also coaxed Donnigan for a garden and he had humored her. But he made her promise that she would allow him to do the hoeing. He was still worried about her and the baby.

Kathleen did not tell Erma about the coming child until midsummer when it was no longer possible to hide her secret. Erma was still grieving over the loss of her own baby. Kathleen believed that her friend should have put aside her grief and her chest of tiny garments before now, but Erma clung to both.

When the truth was finally out, Kathleen saw the hurt look in Erma's eyes. She had so longed to share her joy with her friend but realized that the joy was hers alone. The baby was only a sharp and painful reminder to Erma.

"It seems that I've truly messed up this one," Kathleen scolded herself. "I didn't really get to tell anyone. First I missed sharing it with Donnigan—and that didn't turn out well. Then I couldn't tell Erma until she guessed it herself. I sure do wish there was someone I could tell."

Kathleen thought of Risa, but she had never seemed to be able to form a friendship with the new Mrs. Tremont. Donnigan had even lost touch with Wallis, and Kathleen knew that troubled him. The crusty old bachelor had been good company at one time.

Kathleen longed to be able to share her good news with her own kin. She had tried three times to send a letter to Bridget, but each time it came back to her unopened. It seemed that the country address Kathleen had been given and the school where Bridget was to have attended had never heard of the girl. It worried Kathleen more than she wanted to let show.

The late summer, a warm one, had Donnigan often scolding Kathleen about getting too much sun. She no longer minded his fussing. She realized that it was not because he was viewing her as a child but that he was filled with concern for her and for their coming baby.

So she accepted the good-humored "chastisement" and tried her best to fulfill his wishes.

Harvest time meant that again Donnigan was busy in the fields. But he would no longer allow her the trips with the picnic lunches and water pails. He took his lunch with him, and whenever he was thirsty he stopped at the small creek that ran through the property.

"It's too long a walk. And what if you twisted an ankle on the uneven ground and went down," he worried.

Kathleen only smiled, but she did feel he was unreasonable. Surely she wasn't that clumsy.

He did let her harvest her garden, along with cautions about "overdoing it." Kathleen glowed with pleasure as she took in the vegetables, thinking how much they would improve their diet in the winter months. Some of the produce she canned. Kathleen was sure Donnigan didn't realize what a demanding job it was to spend hours cleaning and preparing the vegetables and then standing over the hot stove processing the canned goods. If he had, he never would have allowed it.

Donnigan had also prepared a root cellar in between his haying and harvesting time. Kathleen was glad to have it ready to accept her garden store.

Eventually the garden and the crops were all properly harvested and stored. Donnigan shared with neighbors in the butchering of hogs and the curing of hams. They were all ready for another winter.

———

Kathleen had been spending her evenings sewing her own tiny baby garments. Never had she enjoyed an activity so much. With each stitch she made she had to push away thoughts of Erma. She was coming to a new understanding of the woman's devastation over her loss. Kathleen found herself counting the days until her own special event.

Even Donnigan seemed to put his fears and concerns a little further from him with each passing month. He dared to hope that things would be fine. While Kathleen sewed, he whittled rungs for a cradle.

"When it is time, I think we should take the stage to Raeford and stay there until the baby comes," Donnigan had informed Kathleen. "That way we will be sure to have a doctor on hand."

Kathleen had not argued. A little trip to the city might

be a nice diversion for both of them.

"What about the farm chores?" she asked instead.

"I'm sure Wallis will watch things for me for a few days," Donnigan responded and it seemed to be settled. Both of the occupants of the household looked forward to what November would bring.

————

"What do you wish to name the baby if it's a girl?" Kathleen asked Donnigan as they breakfasted together one morning.

He hesitated for a moment, then responded with, "What would you suggest?"

"I rather like Meara," said Kathleen.

"Sounds just fine," agreed Donnigan with a nod.

Again silence closed in around them.

" 'Course if it's a boy he'll be named for his father," Kathleen remarked.

His head came up quickly. "You mean Donnigan?"

Kathleen began to chuckle softly. "Of course Donnigan," she said, laying a hand on his arm. "You *are* his father."

He shook his head as he lifted his coffee cup. "No siree," he said emphatically. "No son of mine is gonna carry that handle around for the rest of his life."

Kathleen looked surprised.

"I told you I had to fight my way all through my school days," went on Donnigan. "My boy might have him a fight or two—but it won't be over his name if I can help it."

"What then?" asked Kathleen.

"Something plain and sensible—like Frank or George," he answered.

"I don't like either of those," said Kathleen with a lift of her chin. She decided that she would give the matter of a boy's name some careful thought.

————

Donnigan went alone to town for supplies. The wind was chilly and the sky threatening. Kathleen looked at the gray sky and agreed with her husband that she should stay home. It made her shiver just to look outside.

"When it storms this time of year it could last awhile," Donnigan said with another glance at the sky. "I'd best go on in while I have the chance."

Kathleen nodded and made out her list while Donnigan went for the team.

It was early in the afternoon when Kathleen felt the first uncomfortable twinge. It only lasted for a few minutes and then it was gone. She dismissed it as some strange muscle spasm and went on with her baking.

When it was repeated a few minutes later, she felt some alarm.

"It can't be the baby," she told herself. "He isn't due for three weeks yet."

But in another fifteen minutes, Kathleen had another sharp pain. She looked at the clock, willing Donnigan home.

By the time he did arrive, Kathleen had been forced to take to her bed. Donnigan panicked.

"But you said it wasn't to be until the end of November," he reminded Kathleen.

Kathleen nodded mutely.

"It's only the first part of November," Donnigan said, staring at the calendar on the wall to confirm the fact.

Kathleen nodded again.

"Well—it can't be time—now," Donnigan concluded unreasonably.

"Babies sometimes do things their own way," replied Kathleen, tears in her eyes. She had not planned to be on her own for this delivery, and the very thought of it was frightening.

"What can we do?" he asked her. "The storm has moved in and the doctor is miles away."

"It's too early," moaned Kathleen again. She did wish that her baby would decide to wait until the proper time.

"I'll go for help."

"Go where?" cried Kathleen as another contraction seized her.

"I don't know—but we need *someone*."

Kathleen clung to his arm until the pain subsided.

"Don't go," she pleaded. "I don't want to be alone."

"But we need—" he began.

"Donnigan," she said as calmly as she could manage. "You have helped the stock—many times."

He looked shocked. "You are not stock," he informed her.

"But babies are born the same way," she argued. "Just—just use common sense. We can manage."

In the end it was Donnigan who delivered his son, washed him, and placed him in his mother's arms.

"Now I'm going for the doctor," he informed his pale but happy wife.

"Whatever for?" asked Kathleen, puzzled.

"To make sure everything is all right," he answered her.

"We're fine. Look at him. He's just perfect."

Donnigan looked down at his newborn son. He did look fine. Just wonderful. He was tiny—being early—but he looked wiry and strong.

The fear gradually left Donnigan's eyes—to be replaced with a look of thankfulness and pride. The baby and Kathleen seemed to have made it through the delivery in great form. He lifted a hand to brush his hair back off his glistening brow and took a deep breath.

"So what are you calling him?" he asked as he reached down and gently touched the tiny fingers with his large one.

"Sean," beamed Kathleen. "This is Sean. It is just right for him, don't you think?"

Donnigan nodded. The name sure wasn't Frank or George. Donnigan hoped his son wouldn't have to do too much fighting over it.

———

Kathleen's days were now more than full. Sean was a contented baby, but there were the extra chores that a baby always brings. The laundry was the biggest job. Kathleen found it hard to get things dry in the winter. She would be glad when spring would begin to make its way over the surrounding hillsides and when she would hear the song of the first robin.

————

"Look at him! He'll soon be off on his own," boasted Donnigan as he walked his small son around the kitchen holding only to his fingers.

Kathleen smiled. "He will, and that's the truth of it," she agreed, her voice filled with love and her eyes sparkling with honest pride.

"He's growing so fast," said Donnigan.

Kathleen was silent for a minute. Then her head came up and she spoke with a twinkle in her voice. It was the first Donnigan had heard her thick brogue for many months. "Sure now, and he'd better, I'm thinking. He's going to be a big brother to someone before he knows it."

Donnigan stopped still.

"You're serious?" he asked, watching her face closely.

"I'm serious," she replied, her cheeks warm with the excitement of her news.

Donnigan swung his small son in the air and cheered. "You hear that, my boy?" he asked the baby as he held him above his head. "You are about to be a big brother."

"Hold on," Kathleen laughed. "It won't be for months yet. As I have it figured, Sean will be fifteen months old."

They knew the baby had no idea what the celebration was all about, but they danced around the kitchen with him anyway. Sean laughed at all the merrymaking.

————

Good news came from Erma. Kathleen cried when she read her little note.

"Oh, I do hope it all works out fine for her this time," she said to Donnigan as she blew her nose. "It would be terrible if she lost another."

Kathleen cast a glance at Sean who slept peacefully in the cradle in the corner. He had almost outgrown the bed already—but then it wouldn't be too many months until he would need to pass the cradle on to another. Kathleen smiled to herself. She and Erma were due about the same time.

———

"How will you manage with two babies?" Donnigan asked one morning as Kathleen tried to prepare the porridge while Sean thumped his spoon nosily, calling for his breakfast.

Kathleen attempted a smile. "If they are all as good as that one, I'll have no trouble," she answered.

It was true. Sean had been a model baby. His temperament was such that he was almost always happy. Rarely was he impatient as he seemed to be at the moment.

"I'm late this morning, that's all," Kathleen went on to explain away her son's behavior.

"Aren't you feeling well?" asked Donnigan with concern.

Kathleen shook her head. "Just a little queasiness. It'll pass."

"But you weren't that way at all with Sean," reminded Donnigan. He had been expecting morning sickness, thinking that it went naturally with pregnancy and was surprised when Kathleen had shown no signs.

"It's different—with different babies," said Kathleen lightly. "I remember Madam. She was so sick with Bridget and not a bit with Charles, and then she was sick again with Edmund."

Donnigan nodded, but he still felt nervous about this second baby coming so close to the first one.

———

Without a conscious decision on her part, Kathleen was indeed changing the little cabin, making it into a home.

Perhaps small Sean had a part in the shaping. Baby things now appeared. A small blanket here, a pile of soft garments there, a warm wrap on the rocking chair in the corner to bundle him in while he nursed.

But other things had slowly happened as well. Soft curtains covered the windows. A geranium bloomed in a pot on the kitchen table. Warm rugs were scattered upon the floor. Pictures now broke the bleakness of bare wood walls. And always there was the warm, inviting smell of something cooking or baking or brewing. Donnigan loved to open the door and be welcomed in.

"I'll meet you back at the hotel," Donnigan said as he passed young Sean to Kathleen and moved to tie the team.

Kathleen nodded and they went their separate ways—she to do her shopping and then take tea with Erma, and he to make some necessary purchases at the blacksmith shop.

Kathleen hurried through her errands. She was anxious to spend as much time with Erma as she could. Now that Erma was expecting another baby, Kathleen was not so reluctant to visit her with Sean.

Not that she boasted of her small son—but then, Kathleen did not need to boast. Erma—or anyone—could see for herself what a bright and pleasant baby he was.

Erma was making progress. Oh, she still grieved of the past. She still trembled when speaking of Lucas's dark mood at the loss of their child—as though it had been her fault. She still wept on occasion over the little chest at the foot of her bed—but she also had her cheerier times. She had even smiled slightly on one or two occasions. Kathleen felt encouraged.

"Have you heard from your sis yet?" Erma asked as they sat sipping tea and watching Sean devour a tea biscuit.

"No. I've tried twice more to get a letter off to her—and they both came back again," Kathleen said, her voice filled with despair.

"It's a strange thing, it is," observed Erma, her eyes shadowed.

"I can't understand it at all. I can get my letters to the school headmistress, so the address I was given is correct. But they insist they have never heard of her."

"Oh look!" squealed Erma. "He shoved the whole thing in," and Erma began to chuckle merrily over the small Sean who had pushed such a large bite of biscuit into his mouth that he couldn't even chew.

It was so good to hear Erma laugh again—Kathleen felt like weeping. Instead she went to rescue her small son.

"You little piggy," she scolded gently. "You'll be choking yourself, and that's the truth."

But the laugh had been good for them both.

————

Donnigan's eyes were dark with concern when he met her later on, and Kathleen braced herself to hear whatever bad news he carried.

"Risa is gone," he said.

"Gone? What do you mean, gone?"

"She left. Left on the stage."

Kathleen could only stare. She knew by Donnigan's face that he wasn't teasing.

"Did Wallis go?" she asked in a half whisper.

"Wallis? No. Not Wallis," replied Donnigan.

"How—? What happened?"

"I don't know. Sam only knows that she left—and that Wallis is nearly beside himself."

Kathleen shifted the small Sean to her other arm. "That's terrible," she responded. "What can we do?"

"I've no idea—but I'd like to get home as quick as we can. I'll have to go over and see Wallis."

Chapter Seventeen

Understanding

It was true. Risa had left Wallis. She had gone to town to shop—she said—and not returned. Wallis went to look for her and was told that she had caught the two-o'clock stage heading east. Risa had talked to no one but the ticket agent. "She said she was going to Raeford to catch the train," said the man. "Thet's all I know."

"But why?" wailed Wallis. "Why?"

Donnigan spent some time with his old friend, letting him talk, hearing him out, offering his help.

"Shore, we had our times," admitted Wallis, wiping at unashamed tears. "All couples do I guess. But they weren't of much importance—an' they didn't last fer long."

Donnigan nodded. He and Kathleen had experienced their "times" as well. It took a good deal of adjusting to get things worked out in a marriage. There were still occasions when they seemed to look at the same situation with two different sets of eyes.

"She came from a big city. Didn't care much fer the farm. She called it dirty an' a weed patch," went on Wallis. He sniffed forlornly. "I thought we was gettin' things whipped into pretty good shape."

Wallis stopped to look around his little cabin and Donnigan's eyes followed his. The room bore the marks of a woman's hands. An edge of lace curtain hung at the sparkling window. The cupboard shelves were covered with a ruffle of

157

blue gingham. Woven rugs were scattered across the floor, and the crude table's cracks were hidden by an oil cloth with sprays of bright yellow flowers. It certainly didn't look like the cabin Donnigan remembered. With a wry grin he noticed that there were no bridles or pieces of harness anywhere. Not on the pegs by the door—not on the chairs. Not even on the floor in the corner.

It was Donnigan who put on the coffeepot. Wallis didn't seem to be thinking too well. He hadn't eaten since he'd had the news.

Donnigan wished he could say, "She'll be back," but he wasn't sure if it was true.

Instead he said, "We'll see what we can find out. Surely there is some way to trace her. Find out just why—what it was that—" He didn't know how to say it. Didn't know how to go on with his thoughts. Wallis didn't seem to even notice.

Wallis looked up at the smell of the boiling coffee. Donnigan went to the cupboard and found some bread and jam. It wasn't much but it might get the man through the day.

But Wallis just looked at the bread and his face crumpled again. "She sure could bake good bread," he said to Donnigan and the tears were running down his cheeks again.

Donnigan supposed that the next days would hold many memories for Wallis. It seemed that everywhere he looked there were reminders of Risa's presence in the home.

At length Donnigan faced the fact that there was really nothing more he could do for the grieving man, and he had a pack of chores waiting for him at home. He bid Wallis goodnight with the promise that he'd be back the next day.

"How is he?" asked Kathleen.

Donnigan's shoulders slumped in discouragement. He took off his broad hat and ran a hand through his hair. "He's pretty badly shaken up," he said wearily.

"I know—I know it must have been hard for her. But how

could she do that to him?" said Kathleen, anger edging her voice.

"I don't think Risa was ever happy there—and you must admit that Wallis wouldn't be an easy man to live with."

"No man is easy to live with," said Kathleen.

"Even me?" he quipped.

But she was in no mood for teasing. He knew that her anger had to have vent. He only smiled to himself. Kathleen still had trouble with her temper.

"That doesn't give one call to—to just pack up and leave," Kathleen went on.

"No. No," agreed Donnigan, "it wasn't fair for her to just leave—without—without giving the man a chance—without saying her piece—or even saying goodbye. It wasn't a good way to be doing it."

He pushed his fingers through his hair again. "I need to get to the chores," he said, weariness tinging his voice again.

"I slopped the pigs and fed the hens," said Kathleen.

His eyes dropped to her waistline and Kathleen could read his thinking. "Kathleen—I wish you wouldn't—" He was trying to shelter her again.

"I didn't fill the pails to the top," she argued. "And the pigs were squealing for their supper. And I had to go to the chicken pen to gather the eggs anyway."

Donnigan nodded, but his thoughts were still heavy as he left the house. He ached for Wallis. The poor man was grieving as if he had faced a death. And maybe he had. How could a man lose what was a part of him and not feel that something—something real and important had died? And what on earth would he ever do if something happened to his Kathleen?

———

"Sure now, and that boy's not an Irishman," Kathleen commented as she and Donnigan watched their small son playing on the floor. "He's even fairer than his father."

Sean squealed as he batted at the new red ball that Donnigan had brought home from town.

"Well, he doesn't have an Irish temper—and that's the pure truth," teased Donnigan and got the response that he had expected as a towel Kathleen was folding came flying through the air.

He caught it and tossed it back, grinning in playfulness.

Kathleen sobered. "You're right," she admitted. "He's never had a temper fit."

"Well, he is all of nine months old," Donnigan reminded her.

"Sure—and a good Irish baby can be mighty good at screaming by nine months," responded Kathleen, and they both laughed.

"I wonder what this new one will be like?" Kathleen wondered softly.

"You expect it to be different?"

The ball rolled away and Sean chased it across the floor and caught up to it under a kitchen chair. Donnigan watched as the small boy maneuvered his way between the legs and rungs to retrieve what he was after.

"He's smart," he boasted to the child's mother.

"Sure now—and that's Irish," laughed Kathleen.

Donnigan turned back to his wife. "You really expect the next one to be different?"

"Well . . ." said Kathleen slowly as she lifted the laundry basket. "I've never met two people exactly alike yet. And from what I'm knowing—they mostly start out like they are going to be from the very beginning."

Donnigan nodded.

Kathleen let her eyes return to her infant son, love and pride glowing in them. "If the good Lord sent another one just like him—I wouldn't be complaining," she said and she started toward the bedroom with her clean laundry.

There were clouds in the afternoon sky. Kathleen wondered if Donnigan might get rained on. He was working the far field and was a long ways from the shelter of the house.

"I think it's going to rain," she said to the small boy who had pulled himself up to a kitchen chair and was playing with a ball of Kathleen's mending yarn. "Your father might get wet."

Sean gurgled and grinned.

"You're not worried?" Kathleen gently scolded. "Well, I guess I shouldn't worry either. He is a big man—he can take care of himself."

But in spite of her words, Kathleen found her eyes kept going back to the window and the approaching storm.

Then the thunder began to roll in the distance and sheets of lightning danced across the darkened sky.

"It's going to rain for sure," said Kathleen to her son. "I wish he would come in."

But Kathleen knew that Donnigan would likely stay in the field for as long as he could—fighting to beat the rain.

The storm moved in rapidly. The thunder now cracked and crackled overhead. The lightning zigzagged across the sky, ripping open the dark, tumbling clouds. Kathleen waited for the sound of rain, but there was only the angry thunder and the slashing, rending light.

An unusually loud crash of thunder shook the little cabin and Sean looked bewildered, then frightened, and his lip curled and he began to cry. Kathleen crossed quickly to him and scooped him into her arms.

"That was a close one and that's for sure," she said as she rocked the wee babe in her arms and tried to soothe him. Inside, her own stomach was churning with fright. She had never been in a storm that had struck so close. She did wish that Donnigan would hurry.

She crossed back to the window to peer out and see if he might be coming, but a frightening sight met her eyes. The nearby haystack was in flames.

"Oh, merciful God!" cried Kathleen, "we've been hit."

She wasn't sure what to do. She was thankful that the stack was far enough away from the barn and corrals that it shouldn't be a concern.

"Oh, Donnigan," she cried as she clutched Sean. "Hurry!"

And then, to Kathleen's horror she saw the little fingers of hungry flames that were reaching out from the stack and igniting grass as it moved from the stack to the ground around. The rivulets of flame were moving directly toward the house. Kathleen clutched Sean closer. What should she do? Flee—or fight?

Without time for more thought, Kathleen hurriedly placed her son on the floor and ran from the cabin. She stopped only long enough to grab a gunny sack from the nearby root cellar and dip it in the trough, then hurried toward the flames. Each time that she beat one back, another seemed to stream toward her. The heat from the burning stack was almost more than she could bear. But she had to save her home. She had to save her son.

Tears streamed down her face as she fought on. They were the only moisture with which she fought—for the rains had still not come.

"Oh, God!" cried Kathleen. "God help me. Help me."

But even as she cried she feared that it was a losing battle. The flames that reached toward the cabin seemed to be stronger than the frail woman who fought against them.

Just as she was about to faint from her exertion, the heavens opened and the rain came pouring down. Kathleen lifted her eyes to the darkened skies and cried a thank you, then returned to her fight with renewed determination. With the help of the rain, she should be able to win her war.

"Kathleen. Kathleen!"

Kathleen heard his call but she didn't answer. She didn't stop beating at the flames that were now slowly retreating.

"Kathleen," he said and he grabbed her shoulders and pulled her toward him.

Kathleen's face was white except for the streaks of dirty gray from the soot that floated around her. Her hair was dishevelled, her dress torn at the hem. She was drenched from head to toe with the rain she had prayed for, and her eyes were so filled with terror that she looked like a wounded thing—caught in a trap from which she could not flee.

Donnigan pulled her close for one brief minute and held her. "It's all right," he tried to comfort her but his own body was shaking. "The rain will stop it. It's all right."

He smoothed her hair back from her face and then moved his hands to hold her head, touching the dirty cheeks with his thumbs.

"It's all right now," he comforted again.

Kathleen nodded dumbly, the tears mixing freely with the rain on her face.

"You go in," he said. "See to Sean. I'll watch this."

Kathleen noticed that he was soaked through. Near the barn the team stood—in harness and untethered. Donnigan never left the horses like that.

Then Kathleen thought of her young son. He had been terrified by the storm. What would he be feeling now, being dumped quickly on the floor while his mother fled the house? He must be frightened half to death being left alone in the cabin.

Kathleen took one more look at Donnigan then moved from his arms.

She found her son halfway between the house and the burning stack. He had been crying. His eyes were still red and puffy, but now he sat, playing quite happily in a puddle of muddy water. The rain still washed over him, soaking his clothing, running over his blond hair, and dripping from his chin. From time to time he stuck out his tongue to try to catch the drops; then he returned to splashing the dirty water from the puddle up and over his clothes—over his face.

He squealed when he saw Kathleen coming and his hand slapped more excitedly in the puddle, making the muddied water fly even faster.

Kathleen began to cry. Then to laugh. "Look at you!" she exclaimed. "How did you get here?"

She picked up her rain-drenched son and looked toward the house. The door was wide open. Sean could not open doors. Donnigan had not been to the house. That meant only one thing. In her hurry, she had left the door open.

Kathleen hugged Sean close. "You could have been hurt,"

she murmured. "You could have been burned. I wouldn't even have seen you in my concern for the fire."

Again Kathleen lifted her head heavenward. She had something more for which to be thankful.

———

The next day she lost the baby she was carrying. The pains had started during the night. There was really nothing they could do to stop it from happening. When it was all over, Kathleen turned her face to the wall and cried uncontrollable tears. She had wanted the baby. Another little Sean. She had already learned to love him. Had been counting the months.

"We have Sean," Donnigan whispered, wiping away her tears.

But suddenly that didn't seem to be enough. She had wanted them both. Had wanted both of her babies to love and care for. One couldn't make up for the loss of the other. It wasn't that simple.

For the first time, Kathleen felt she truly understood Erma's pain. No wonder the woman had grieved. It wasn't just "hope" that she had lost. It was a child. A child she had carried, had loved. Kathleen sobbed for the baby she would never know.

It was a long time until she could fall asleep.

———

"Kathleen?" The voice was low and gentle. It was Donnigan. Kathleen waited until the voice came again. "Kathleen?"

She stirred to let him know she had heard him.

"How are you?" he asked and dropped beside her on the bed, smoothing back her hair, letting his fingers trace her cheek.

"Where's Sean?" she asked, rather than answering his question.

"Sleeping. He's fine."

He continued to brush back her long dark hair.

"Would you like some supper?"

Kathleen shook her head. She had no desire for something to eat.

"Tea? You should take something."

"Not tonight," said Kathleen, and Donnigan did not push further.

There was heavy silence in the room. Donnigan seemed to be battling with his thoughts—or how to say his words.

"Would—would you like to see—see your daughter?" he finally managed, his voice choked.

Kathleen's eyes widened. She hadn't thought about the baby's gender—nor the possibility of seeing her miscarried child.

She tried to swallow—but her throat didn't work well. She felt the tears sting her eyes. She wanted to answer Donnigan but the words would not come. So she just nodded her head, mutely.

Donnigan brushed at one of the tears on her cheek. "You—you must remember that it—it won't be like seeing Sean—for the first time," Donnigan said softly and Kathleen knew he was trying to prepare her. Shelter her again. Love swelled her heart. She felt that Donnigan would go through life trying to shelter her. She was glad.

"She's very small," continued Donnigan. "And she isn't—isn't like a newborn—exactly. But she's all there. Even her little fingers. Her toes."

Kathleen knew now without a doubt that she wanted to see her baby. Had to see her baby. "Bring her to me," she whispered.

Donnigan let his fingers trail across her cheek, rub her hair, and then he rose from the bed and left the room.

He carried the little bundle to its mother in the palm of one of his big hands. He had bathed the tiny body and wrapped her in a soft face cloth. She was far too tiny to dress in any of the small baby garments.

He did not lay her in Kathleen's arms as he had done

with Sean, but lowered his hand so that Kathleen could look at her child. And yes, she was all there. Even those tiny little fingers that Donnigan had spoken of.

"There *must* be a God in heaven," Kathleen breathed as she reached a finger out to gently touch the tiny hand, and the tears began to flow again, unchecked.

"Put her in my hands," said Kathleen when she could speak, and Donnigan gently eased the little body into the hands of the sobbing mother. "I—I would have called her Taryn," said Kathleen through her tears.

"Taryn," repeated Donnigan. "I like it. Taryn."

And both of them knew that Taryn she would always be.

"I've made a little—little casket," said Donnigan, his voice deep with emotion. "I used that cedar handkerchief box from the dresser. I lined it with some of the flannel from your sewing basket."

"Oh, Donnigan," wailed Kathleen as she suddenly leaned against him. "I wanted her so much. So much."

Donnigan held her and they wept together. Then Donnigan gently retrieved the small burden from Kathleen's hands.

"I thought—under the tree at the end of the garden," he said softly. "She'll always be with us then."

Kathleen was weeping into her pillow.

"I'll bring her in before I go."

As promised, Donnigan brought the baby in for her mother to see one last time. She looked like a tiny sleeping doll arranged on the white flannel, the folds gently tucked about her elfin face. The cedar hankie box was plenty big enough. Kathleen was glad that Donnigan had thought of it.

In the morning, the tree at the end of the garden sheltered a small mound of freshly dug earth. Later Donnigan made a small wooden cross, and on it, with his whittling knife, he carved a tiny rosebud. "For our little bud that never became a flower," he told Kathleen, and brought the tears to her eyes again.

Chapter Eighteen

Fiona

Wallis continued to grieve over Risa. In spite of Donnigan's effort, there was really no way to track the woman. The man who had driven the stage said he had let her off at the Raeford station and that was the last he had seen of her—and yes, she had been carrying a fair amount of luggage.

From sorrow, Wallis eventually turned to anger. He said some nasty things to Donnigan that were not even repeated to Kathleen.

Kathleen had her own grief. Donnigan was reminded of it over and over as he saw the sadness in her eyes when she looked toward the wooden cradle in the corner or smoothed out a tiny baby garment. He noticed the clusters of fresh flowers that were placed almost daily on the little mound at the back of the yard. The little mound that was quickly sinking to take its place with the ground around it.

"We should build a little fence," Kathleen said, and Donnigan put aside his harvest work for a day to fulfill her request.

But Kathleen's grief was no longer voiced. Donnigan felt that it would have been better for her—for both of them—if it was. She wiped away her tears—straightened her back and lifted a stubborn chin.

But part of her seemed withdrawn—shut away—angry. Only with Sean did her old tenderness really return.

"She and Wallis seem to be dealing with the same emotions," Donnigan told Black one day. "And I don't know how to help either one of them."

It was a heavy burden for Donnigan to carry.

———————

For Sean's first birthday, Kathleen made a cake and they invited Wallis to join them for the party. At first he declined but then changed his mind. He had shared a number of supper hours with them since Risa had left him. Kathleen did not mind the crusty old bachelor, though he was slipping back into his former way of living. Kathleen wondered if he had bathed or changed his shirt since Risa had left.

In spite of the heaviness of the hearts around the table, Sean's birthday celebration was a joyous occasion and a success. The boy ate too much cake, stuffing it into his mouth with his fingers while his spoon was held idly in his other hand. The grown-ups laughed at his messy face and Sean responded by beaming back at them.

"He sure is one fine boy," observed Wallis. And then his eyes filled with tears and Kathleen knew he was thinking of Risa again and of the son that he'd never have. Kathleen left the table in pretense of getting more coffee.

"It wasn't fair of Risa," Kathleen fumed to herself. She had made her promise before the God in heaven. She'd really had no right to break it.

———————

"Do you believe in God?"

Donnigan's question caught Kathleen totally off guard. Where had his thoughts been wandering to produce such a query?

"Of course," she replied without hesitation. She didn't see how anyone could *not* believe in a God.

Donnigan remained silent.

"Don't you?" asked Kathleen, having sudden, frightening doubts about her husband.

Donnigan thought before answering. When he did speak it was with honesty. "I've never really given it much thought," he said truthfully. "Not until Taryn died. Then— then I—I really wanted to believe."

Kathleen nodded. Vivid in her own mind was her response to the sight of her small daughter. Her statement that there had to be a God in heaven. Such a tiny little miracle could not just have happened on its own.

Kathleen was still willing to concede the fact. Of course there was a God—somewhere.

But that very admission did not bring her comfort. In fact, it filled her with anger. He was there—somewhere—and if there—then powerful. A God wouldn't be a God unless He had some power. Some authority. So why hadn't He done something? Why had He let the lightning strike the haystack. Why hadn't He brought the rain sooner so that she would not have had to fight so long—and so hard? No. Kathleen was annoyed with God. She wouldn't have dared to admit it—not even to Donnigan—lest she be smitten down and made to pay for her sin. But she felt the anger, regardless.

"I've been thinking a lot lately," Donnigan went on.

Kathleen waited, but when he didn't say anything further she prompted, "About?"

"About Sean—mostly."

Again, silence. Kathleen felt fear tugging at her. What was wrong with Sean?

"It seems—well, it seems if there really is a God—then we ought to be learning about Him—so we can teach Sean," said Donnigan.

Kathleen let out the breath she had been holding.

"What do you think?" asked Donnigan.

It was a direct question that Kathleen could not avoid.

"I—I suppose," she said without really wishing to commit herself.

She knit a few more stitches. She heard the rattle of the newspaper as Donnigan laid it aside.

"I think—the next time I'm in town I'll just check out that little church where we were married," said Donnigan, causing Kathleen's brows to lift in surprise. "Maybe we should start taking in some of the meetings."

Kathleen only nodded. She would not argue—but she really didn't feel ready to go to church, and besides, she saw no advantages in the idea.

Then she looked at her young son.

"Yes—yes," she admitted to herself. "If there really is a God—and there must be—there must be—then I want Sean to know all about Him."

But the next time Donnigan came home from town he looked disappointed.

"They closed the church," he told her.

"What?"

"They closed it. Weren't enough people interested."

"What's the preacher doing now?" asked Kathleen. "Would he open it again?"

"He left. Went off to some other town. No one seems to really know much about it. Weren't that many people attending."

Kathleen felt two emotions at the same time. Disappointment for Donnigan's sake and unexplained fear for the small Sean. She didn't know which feeling was the most intense.

"So what do we do now?" she asked simply.

"Not much we *can* do, I guess," said Donnigan. He hung his stained Stetson on the peg by the door and reached to lift his young son from the floor.

The arrival of Erma's baby was a grim reminder to Kathleen of the baby she had lost. Little Taryn should have been joining the family about the same time—not four and a half months earlier. Kathleen had a hard time fighting renewed sorrow. But she was happy for Erma.

Lucas was having a bit of a struggle. He had definitely

ordered a son. Erma had presented him with a daughter. Blond and dimpled and looking just like her mother. Erma was thrilled, but Lucas seemed confused. For the first time in his life he was dealing with something totally out of his control. First he had lost the child he wanted—then someone had mixed up his order. Poor Lucas. His grip on his world seemed to be slipping from his fingers.

———

Kathleen was expecting another baby. Sean, now two, was quickly becoming more and more like his father. Kathleen smiled as she watched the child follow his father around the farm, trying hard to copy everything he saw Donnigan do.

He enjoyed the farm animals, and Kathleen often took him for rides on Shee. He loved the horse and grinned his delight as soon as Kathleen placed him in the saddle.

"That boy needs a pony of his own," observed Donnigan and promptly set about seeing to it.

"Don't hurry him too fast," cautioned Kathleen. She wasn't yet ready to give up her baby.

But with each passing month, and the new baby on the way, Kathleen was more and more glad for the time that Sean spent with Donnigan. She didn't tell Donnigan about it, for fear she would trouble him unduly, but she did not feel at all well with this pregnancy. She wondered if it was just concern after having lost Taryn.

Slowly the months ticked by and Kathleen began to feel a bit better and breathe a little easier.

"I hope we can have a doctor on hand this time," observed Donnigan as he unlaced his heavy work boots one night.

"Why," teased Kathleen gently. "You did just fine."

"I was scared to death," said Donnigan firmly. "I never want to go through that again."

But he did. Just a few weeks later. There hadn't been time to send for a doctor. Kathleen was early again.

A baby girl was placed in Kathleen's arms. Her first

thought had been, *This can't be mine. There must be a mix-up*. But her own good sense told her that a mix-up was not a possibility.

"She's so—so different than Sean," she said to Donnigan.

"Wasn't that what you said—what you expected?" replied Donnigan. He still looked to be a bundle of nerves, even though it was all over.

"But not *this* different," protested Kathleen. The baby she held was dark. With lots of black hair, round full cheeks, and a face that was already screwed up in protest.

They had decided—or rather Kathleen had decided—on the name Fiona if they had a girl. Now the mother smiled at her daughter. "Hello, Fiona," she said. Then to Donnigan, "Fiona suits her, don't you think?"

"It's going to be fun having a daughter," said Donnigan, and he moved closer to Kathleen and his new baby girl.

———

But it was not fun. Not for the first five months. It seemed to Kathleen that Fiona fussed without stopping. Their days, their evenings, their nights were all filled with a crying baby. Donnigan tried to share the duties, but even with the two of them, it was a full-time chore.

Kathleen thought that surely Sean must resent his new baby sister, but Sean seemed to accept her just as she was. "Baby cry," he would say without rancor, just as though the small boy accepted that was what babies did.

But there were days when Kathleen wondered how much more she could take.

They took the baby off breast milk and tried a bottle. Still Fiona curled into a ball and screamed her protest.

"Her little tummy must be hurting something awful," observed her patient father. There were times when Kathleen wished the infant were big enough to spank. But even at times of greatest distress and weariness, Kathleen knew that was not the solution. There was something wrong with the child and no one seemed to be able to do anything about it.

One day Donnigan surprised Kathleen with a goat.

"Whatever are we to do with that?" asked Kathleen, thinking that Donnigan had likely brought the animal as a pet for Sean. His own "wee" cow. But to the weary Kathleen, the nanny looked like just another chore.

"Milk her," said Donnigan.

"Milk her? We scarcely have time to milk the cow."

"For Fiona," went on Donnigan. "I've heard that sometimes it works."

And it did. After being switched to goat's milk, Fiona settled down and became a laughing, bubbling, good-humored baby. Kathleen even got to sleep nights. The household returned to a normal pattern.

"Bless that nanny," Kathleen said to Donnigan one night as she carefully tucked the covers up to the chin of the sleeping Fiona. Then she lifted her head and smiled at her husband. "And bless you for finding the solution."

"I had to," said Donnigan with a teasing grin. "It was either that—or move out."

———

Fiona grew quickly. Even Sean enjoyed her sunny disposition—as long as she didn't interfere with his time with his father.

But Sean did take care of her. Bringing her things that she should not have—things like his bread crusts, Kathleen's sewing scissors, and wiggling worms from the garden. Kathleen had to ever be on guard to intercept Sean's "gifts" to his baby sister.

Kathleen was pleased with her little family. As she became rested again, she was able to really enjoy the two children in spite of the amount of work that had come with them. She almost got to the place where she could forgive God. That is, until she looked at the little grave with its white picket fence and tiny wooden cross.

———

If Donnigan was in the barn or working around the yard, Kathleen did not have to concern herself with her small son. He was always following close to his father. He went with Donnigan to care for the horses, slop the pigs, or milk the cow. He watched him hoe the garden, lift water from the well, and chop the wood. Then he tried with all of the strength of his small body to imitate his father's acts. Donnigan found himself taking extra precautions. He made sure the corral gate was carefully closed. He didn't want a small boy under the hooves of the horses. He latched the barn door and double checked. He didn't want Sean kicked by a nervous cow. He secured the well lid, added a second clip that he always put in place. He hung the hoe high above the small boy's head. Donnigan was very conscious of the small lad who was watching him—copying him.

But in spite of all of Donnigan's care, an accident did happen.

Wallis had borrowed one of Donnigan's axes. In coming to call one evening he had spotted a tree down on his fence wires. It was closer to go on to Donnigan's than to go back home for his own axe. Donnigan got his axe from the woodshed and Wallis took care of the matter. Donnigan thought nothing of it when Wallis came to the door later.

"I put yer axe back," the man said and Donnigan nodded and invited the man in.

It was while they were having their coffee that they heard the young boy scream. Donnigan was the first to his feet. Kathleen was just behind him.

Sean was seated on the ground, the axe still in his hand, his small foot oozing blood.

"Oh, merciful Lord," cried Kathleen.

Donnigan scooped up the crying child and headed for the house. Wringing her hands in her apron, Kathleen followed. Wallis could only stand and stare, chiding himself for leaving the axe in the chopping block.

It turned out that it was not a deep cut—but it did cause

much concern. Kathleen feared that it might develop blood poisoning, and Donnigan used some of the same strong disinfectant that he used for the stock to assure that it wouldn't happen. Even though it was diluted, it stung sharply and the small boy cried even louder. Fiona, in her cradle in the corner of the room, heard the cries and joined the bedlam.

Kathleen longed to hold and rock her son, but he clung to his father. She knew she would have to wait her turn. Instead she went to lift the small Fiona from her bed.

Chapter Nineteen

Brenna

When Fiona was a laughing, teasing two-year-old and Sean a four-and-a-half-year-old copy of his father, another baby girl joined the family, aided by the doctor who actually made it on time. Kathleen named her Brenna and Fiona managed to call her Bwee. She was another blond baby but she had more of Kathleen's features than did Sean.

"Now you're getting it right," teased Donnigan. "A little of both of us." Kathleen just smiled.

Sean and Fiona fell in love with their baby sister at once, but it was generally left to Fiona to do the mothering as Sean was much too busy being a "farm man."

A few months later, Erma also had another baby and this one too was a girl, much to Lucas's further consternation. But his oldest girl was busy working on her daddy's heart, and though Lucas might not have admitted it, she had won him over totally. Erma shared the little tales of the doting papa with Kathleen and they both chuckled over them. Lucas tried so hard to convince everyone that he was totally and completely "all business."

Brenna was a contented baby, for which Kathleen was thankful. With two other small children to care for, her days were more than full. Sean took over the task of gathering the eggs and feeding the chickens. It was his first step toward becoming a farmer.

But the garden always needed attention, and the pile of

soiled baby laundry always loomed larger than the clean stock in the chest of drawers. It seemed to Kathleen that there was never time for rest. She was glad that her little brood was healthy and happy.

Brenna was now seven months old, sitting by herself and crawling all over the house. Donnigan was pleased with her progress, as he had been with each of his children. But Kathleen carried a nagging, frightening concern. The baby's eyes were often crossed as she tried to focus on what she held in her hands.

Kathleen, herself raised with a handicap that had not been properly cared for, knew how devastating it could be. Why, if Donnigan had not accepted her "sight unseen," she still didn't know if any man would have ever married her. Her stepmum had thoroughly convinced her that she had an abnormality that no man would be able to overlook. Kathleen did not want any such handicap for one of her children.

Donnigan had helped her limp by making a lift for her boot. In fact, Kathleen hardly thought of her lameness anymore, and certainly Donnigan never made mention of it. But crossed eyes could hardly be hidden under swishing skirts. Brenna's disability would be plain for all to see. So Kathleen fretted and worried and tried to make peace with the God she had been angry with so that she might evoke His intervention. Each day she watched the little eyes as they concentrated on what was held in the small hands, and still they crossed on occasion.

Kathleen kept waiting for Donnigan to speak of it, but Donnigan either did not notice or refused to admit what he saw. It annoyed Kathleen. Wasn't he concerned about his baby?

At last she had to bring it up. "What can we do about Brenna?" was the way she approached him.

"What about Brenna?" he asked innocently, and Kathleen stirred restlessly, her temper immediately roused.

"Her eyes?" she said with a bit too much emphasis.

"What's wrong with her eyes?"

Now Kathleen was really upset. "Don't tell me," she began, "that you haven't even noticed that your daughter has crossed eyes?"

"What?" he answered, his tone even and controlled in spite of her sharpness. "You mean when she holds something?"

When Kathleen did not answer, Donnigan went on. "All babies do that. They outgrow it as soon as the muscles strengthen."

Kathleen snorted. "And now you are an authority on all babies. Sean didn't do that. Fiona didn't do that."

"Sure they did," argued Donnigan.

"Not when they were as old as Brenna," debated Kathleen.

"So she's a bit slower in that area," said Donnigan, refusing to get concerned.

Kathleen said nothing more. She was still worried about her baby, but it seemed Donnigan did not share her fear.

"We'll keep an eye on her," said Donnigan. "If she doesn't quickly outgrow it, we'll take her to a doctor in Raeford."

"Outgrow it by *when*?" asked Kathleen, wishing for something definite.

"By a year," said Donnigan.

It seemed much too long to wait to Kathleen, but it had to do. She would watch Brenna carefully and then make Donnigan keep his promise when she was a year old.

But Brenna outgrew her difficulty in focusing long before she reached her first birthday. Kathleen breathed a sigh of relief—but was just a bit annoyed that Donnigan had been right—again.

———

"There's a letter for you," Donnigan said as he entered the house, a box of groceries in his arms. Sean tagged along behind him, carrying a small box just like his father.

"Can'ny?" called Fiona, running to meet them. "Can'ny?"

Donnigan laughed and hoisted her up in his arms. "I think your mama might find a bit of candy in there some place—you little sweet tooth, you. Maybe your mama will let you have *one* now—and put the rest up to share later."

He pinched her chubby cheek and returned her to the floor.

"A letter?" said Kathleen, moving forward. She never got letters. Oh, she did hope that it was from Bridget.

The letter bore a strange address but it was from London. Kathleen tore it open with trembling fingers, then quickly let her eyes run down the page until they fell on the signature.

"Why, it's from Edmund," she said, and immediately felt concern. Why would Edmund be the family member to finally get in touch?

"I'll catch it later—I have to care for the team," said Donnigan, to which Sean parroted, "I hafta care for the team," and the two left the house together.

Kathleen wondered if Donnigan instinctively knew that she needed to be alone to read whatever the letter contained of news from home. She sat down on the nearby kitchen chair and opened the letter, totally forgetting about Fiona, who had climbed on another chair and was busily going through the grocery box in search of the promised candy.

My dearest sister Kathleen:

Kathleen smiled to herself. It seemed strange for the spoiled Edmund to be addressing her in such a fashion. Then she read on.

It has been some time since you left London to make your new home in America. Bridget tried for some time to get in touch but was unable to secure your address.

"Oh, Bridget," sobbed Kathleen, "I tried so hard to contact you."

She has since married and is living quite happily in

Belfast. The man she married is an Irishman with much concern for his homeland.

The word "his" had been crossed out and Edmund had inserted instead the word "our." Again Kathleen smiled. Edmund had never evidenced much love for Ireland. Indeed, Madam had seen that his loyalties were more toward France.

Charles left two years ago to join up with a cargo ship. It nearly broke Mere's heart. I would have thought that he could find himself a trade nearby. We have heard from him a few times since, but mostly his days are spent at sea.

So there is now just Mere and me, and our situation is rather distressful. You may wonder why we are in London. The marriage that was planned didn't take place. He proved to be a scoundrel. We shall never forgive him. At any rate, we have continued on in the city but were forced to leave the house on Carrington when we couldn't manage the rent.

Mere is pleased that she sent you to America where you were able to better your situation by marrying a man of means.

"Sent me?" sniffed Kathleen in disbelief.

Even though your going put great stress on the family here, we gladly sacrificed for your betterment. Now we are hoping that our charity will be returned. Whatever you might spare would be most appreciated.

Affectionately, your brother Edmund.

Kathleen sat staring at the page, unable to believe what she had just read. Tears formed in her eyes. It was good to hear from them—to learn that they were well. She thought of her young sister, now a married woman and back home again in beloved Ireland. And she thought of Charles at sea. Imagine that! Charles, a sailor. Perhaps on his way to becoming a captain. Kathleen smiled and wiped at her cheeks.

Fiona had found the bag of licorice and climbed down from her chair. She sat on the floor, out of view of her mother, and began to enjoy her treat. She had eaten three of the pieces before she thought of Brenna. Brenna was sitting on the floor happily playing with two of her mama's pots. Fiona picked a candy from her sack and stuffed it in the baby's mouth. It was not easy for the baby to chew, and the whole dribbling, sloppy mess soon tumbled out of her mouth again and trickled down the front of her gown. The licorice lodged in a fold in her lap. Brenna smacked her lips a few times and returned to her pots. Fiona, feeling she had shared adequately, went back to enjoying her treat. Kathleen still sat at the table, wiping her eyes and blowing her nose.

In spite of her joy in receiving news from home, she felt annoyance. "My, what a fine kettle of fish that must have been, and that's the truth," she muttered to herself as she scanned the page again. "No marriage. A scoundrel was he? And why not, I'm thinking. It takes one to draw one."

Kathleen had never dared to dwell on her feelings for her stepmother before. Now they rose up within her, surprising even her with their intensity. So the marriage for wealth had not worked. My, couldn't she just picture the anger of Madam.

Then a new thought occurred to Kathleen. "Why, if I hadn't left *how* I did, *when* I did, I'd still be there making pennies hawking buns and pastries in the dirty London streets," she murmured to herself.

A wave of thankfulness flooded through her. What she had left was so inferior to what she had gained. She closed her eyes tightly and let the emotion sweep over her whole body. What if—? What if she had never signed on to come to America? What if she had never married Donnigan?

She would still be poor and destitute and slaving for a family who did not even think to appreciate her services. She would still be limping around on a lame leg, her back aching at the end of the day, her mind convinced that she was a cripple that no one would want.

She wouldn't have a husband. She wouldn't have a family. She would know nothing about love. She— Kathleen stopped and opened her eyes to survey the family that had blessed her life. Fiona stood before her.

"A' done," she said with great satisfaction, passing Kathleen an empty sack. Licorice stains colored her chin and browned the front of her dress with ugly streaks. Kathleen gasped. "A' done," the girl repeated, dropping the bag in Kathleen's lap.

"You ate them all?" gasped Kathleen.

"No," said Fiona, shaking her head emphatically. "I give Bwee."

Kathleen gasped and jumped to her feet, fearful that she would find the baby passed out on the floor, choked by licorice candy. But Brenna was cooing to herself and fumbling with the pots. All around her mouth and dripping down her front was the evidence of the licorice she never got to fully enjoy. Kathleen breathed a sigh of relief that she was all right and hurried to clean up the pair of them before their father returned from the barn.

———

"You are welcome to read it for yourself," Kathleen told Donnigan as she nodded toward the letter on the small table.

Donnigan shifted the two children on his knees and picked up the letter. He read it all the way through, then read it again. Kathleen waited for his response as she moved about the kitchen getting the supper on the table.

"Sounds like they have fallen into hard times," said Donnigan at last.

Kathleen didn't dare make a response.

"How much do you think we can spare?" was Donnigan's next comment.

Kathleen looked up. Was he serious? Was he actually thinking that Kathleen owed something to Madam?

"Donnigan. Madam has always been in 'hard times'—only before she had Father—or me—to pay her way. I owe her nothing more. Nothing. Why, if she'd had her way I would still be there, walking those London streets, selling wares for that crotchety old baker."

Donnigan had never heard such bitterness in Kathleen's voice before.

He said nothing more—for the moment—but switched his attention to giving his two small daughters horsey rides on his foot.

————

When Donnigan felt that Kathleen had enough time to cool down, he brought up the matter of the letter again.

"I was thinking that we might spare a bit," he said. "We've got that extra pig money in the bank."

"If you start sending money to Madam, she'll expect it as her due," warned Kathleen.

"She *is* kin," replied Donnigan evenly.

"No kin of mine—she simply married my father—and sent my grandmother to an early grave," said Kathleen hotly.

"Your grandmother?" Donnigan had never heard that story.

"Sure now—and Grandmother O'Malley left Ireland when we did and settled with us in London. She cared for me after my mother died. Called me her little colleen. We would have been just fine too had not Madam taken a shine to my father. She worked in the local pub and he used to stop by for a pint after his day's work.

"Before long she had convinced him they should marry—and I guess he was lonely without Mother. But she couldn't leave Grandmother be. She taunted and tormented and picked on her all the time that Father was at work. Then at end of day when Father came home, she was nice as cream pudding to the old lady. I saw it all myself. Of course, Grandmother never said a thing. She didn't want to come between a man and his wife. But it broke her heart, and that's the truth of it. She just gave up and died—pining for my mother—pining for Ireland. I saw it myself."

Kathleen stopped for a breath. Donnigan reached out an arm and drew her close.

"It was hard for you, wasn't it?" he said, but it was more a statement than a question.

Kathleen found that she was crying. She had never talked to anyone about her grandmother before.

Donnigan let her cry against him. When she finally moved to dry her eyes and blow her nose, he spoke again.

"Is it too hard to forgive?" he asked her.

Kathleen sniffed and thought a moment.

"You think she deserves my forgiveness?" she asked stiffly.

"I was thinking of you—not her," said Donnigan. "Unforgiveness is a heavy load to carry."

Kathleen looked up in surprise.

"You had no choice—in what she did to you," went on Donnigan slowly, "but you do have a choice in forgiving."

"One doesn't just decide to forgive—and make it happen," said Kathleen with feeling. "You can't just—will pain away. It goes far deeper than that."

Donnigan nodded. "But somehow I think that you can choose to hang on to pain—to bitterness—sorta cling to it and coddle it and pamper it a bit so that it grows and grows."

Kathleen had never thought of that.

"Would you like to talk about it later?" asked Donnigan, and Kathleen nodded her head.

Donnigan saw it as the first positive step.

Chapter Twenty

The Continued Search

Kathleen was not looking forward to the time when Donnigan might again approach her about sending help home to Madam. She had not realized how deep her bitterness ran until she had looked at her life with the London family in light of her life with Donnigan.

"I guess I just took it all for granted when I was there," she told herself. "When you're used to a situation, you don't realize that things should be different. You just—just accept them."

But now that Kathleen had enjoyed a taste of a real home, of real love, she realized just how much she had been taken advantage of as a child and how Madam had used her for her own purposes.

Kathleen had been unaware of the bitterness she had buried concerning the grandmother she had lost when she was seven years old. It had been bad enough to lose her mother, but she'd still had her Granny to cling to. But when she lost her grandmother as well, she lost her anchor in a hostile world.

Her father had been quite unaware of what went on in the little house in his absence. Yet he should have been able to see that something was dreadfully wrong.

To Kathleen's surprise, she found that buried very deeply within herself was a resentment toward her father. The father she had loved so much. That was perhaps what pained her most of all. And it all was due to Madam. She had forced Kathleen's father into the position where he was not free to properly care for his eldest daughter. Still he should have seen. He should have sensed that things were all wrong. Kathleen felt that she could have forgiven the woman of all the sins that she had committed against her—except that one. The one of making her see her beloved father as a less than perfect man.

Kathleen struggled with her pain and bitterness, and Donnigan wisely didn't press. He knew she wasn't ready.

They needed more room to house their growing family. Donnigan decided he could put it off no longer. He began to order and stockpile the materials so that he could begin at the first opportunity.

"What you plannin'?" asked Wallis when he popped by one evening just as they were about to sit down for their supper.

Kathleen moved to the cupboard to get another plate. It seemed to her that Wallis ate more often at her table than he did at his own. But she would not have expressed her feeling to Donnigan.

"Time to add on to this cabin," said Donnigan as he mashed potatoes for Brenna and covered them with gravy. "We're about to burst at the seams."

Wallis nodded, looking around the circle.

"We're going to build a room for me," piped up Sean, grinning as he shared the good news.

Wallis accepted his place at the table.

I may as well set for him every night, thought Kathleen. *Seems he always ends up being here.*

"When you startin'?" asked Wallis as he stabbed a spud with his fork.

"First thing in the morning—I hope," replied Donnigan.

"I got some spare time right now," said Wallis around a bit of liver and onions. "I'll give you a hand."

That's just fine! thought Kathleen sourly. *Now he'll think he is entitled to eat here* three *times a day!*

Then Kathleen caught herself. She was getting awfully testy lately. She wondered that Donnigan could stand living with her. Maybe it was just that another baby was on the way. She hoped she would soon get her emotions back under control.

Kathleen decided not to wait for Donnigan to speak with her. She brought up the matter herself. She hoped that she would be able to keep her composure as she talked.

"About the money," she began, knowing that Donnigan would know what money she was referring to. "I know we don't have much to spare with building on to the house and all, but perhaps we could send a little bit."

"I'll see to it right away," said Donnigan, and she thought she read relief in his eyes.

"But that doesn't mean I've forgiven her," Kathleen could have said. "I've tried, but I can't. But send the money if you like—it'll make you feel better—and I guess I can grant her that much."

But Kathleen did not say the words, so Donnigan did not know what was going on in her heart. Instead she said, "And, Donnigan—when you send the money, would you please ask Edmund to send me Bridget's address?"

"Do you think there's a God?" Donnigan asked Wallis at the dinner table.

I thought he had forgotten about that, thought Kathleen, lifting her head in surprise.

Wallis, too, looked startled. He chewed on his bite of bread and butter, his eyes going darker by the minute. At last he swallowed and said in a mumbled fashion, "Used to. Kinda."

"You mean, you don't anymore?"

"Nope!" said Wallis, and he took another large bite of the slice he held in his hand.

"But if there is a God—and I've got a strong feeling that there must be—then He doesn't just come and go according to how we feel about Him," Donnigan said rather boldly.

Wallis seemed to be thinking.

"All I know is—if He's there—He sure don't run things very well," said Wallis.

Donnigan nodded. He knew Wallis was thinking about Risa.

"Do you really think *He* had a say in the matter?" he asked softly.

"Well—a God is supposed to be a God, isn't He?" declared Wallis, and there was pain and bitterness in his voice. "What good is He iffen He can't look after things?"

"Maybe it's not His business to look after *those* kinds of things," said Donnigan.

Kathleen was uncomfortable with the conversation. She rose from the table and sliced more bread.

"Then what is He supposed to look after?" asked Wallis, sounding angry and exasperated.

"Our souls," said Donnigan.

Wallis met that comment with a sneer.

"If there's a God—then there is a heaven and hell—somewhere," said Donnigan. "And I think that His business is getting us to the one and keeping us out of the other."

"So how's He do thet?" snorted Wallis.

"I don't know," said Donnigan slowly. "I don't know—but I sure would like to find out."

Kathleen cast a glance Donnigan's way and saw the shadow in his eyes. She knew then that he had not forgotten his search. That he was greatly troubled—somewhere deep inside.

———

The house was finished before the new baby made his

appearance. This boy looked much like his older brother—except that he was dark instead of fair. But from the very first time she heard him cry, Kathleen knew she had a child with a totally different disposition from his brother Sean.

"My, he sounds cross," she said to Donnigan. "Do you think he'll ever forgive the doctor for that pat on his little behind?"

Donnigan had insisted on a doctor again for the birth and Kathleen had not argued. There had been time for the doctor to arrive—although certainly no time to spare.

"He's likely just hungry," replied Donnigan, handing the baby to his mother. "He'll settle down as soon as he's fed."

Kathleen named the baby Eamon, and Donnigan accepted the name without comment.

———

Wallis was back far more often than Kathleen would have liked, but she bit her tongue and served him his suppers whenever he made his sudden appearance at her door.

"He needs us," said Donnigan with real feeling for the neighbor man, and Kathleen did not try to argue.

———

"The more I see of youngsters the less confident I feel as a parent," Donnigan observed one day just after Eamon had thrown a real temper fit.

Kathleen nodded. She was so weary of fighting the two-year-old. It seemed that Eamon was always upset about something.

"He sure isn't like the others," she commented in return, brushing back the hair from her flushed face.

"I think we're going to have our hands full with that one," went on Donnigan, "and I'm not sure just how to handle him. Now, if he was a colt and acted like that I'd try gentling, and if that didn't work I'd lay my whip on him."

Kathleen winced. It seemed to her that Eamon had already been spanked more than his fair share.

"They are all so different," said Kathleen, and reviewed in her mind her four youngsters. Sean was the easiest one. Never had he fussed and fought against their authority. He had immediately fallen in love with his father and sought to do everything just as Donnigan did.

Fiona was the spirited one. Bubbly and chattering and always on the go. She mothered and fussed over each family member and giggled and romped her way through each day.

Brenna was a loner. From the time she was little she could entertain herself for hours, sitting off in a corner or under the table, playing with whatever simple thing Kathleen gave her. She hummed little songs to herself and smiled her pleasure at family members. But then she promptly returned to her play without even asking to be picked up.

But Eamon. Eamon was out to conquer the world on his own terms even before he took his first step. Kathleen shared Donnigan's concern for their youngest son. She had no idea how to handle him.

"We need help, Kathleen," said Donnigan, and he looked weary, concerned. "I'm not smart enough to know how to raise my little ones fit for heaven, and I admit it."

There it was again. Donnigan's concern for the soul.

"I wish there was a church—"

Donnigan ran his fingers through his heavy head of blond hair.

"I don't think they're *that* bad," said Kathleen, defending her young.

"It's not a case of how good or how bad, Kathleen. I don't know what God wants. I don't know how to prepare my children for—for the world to come. There's no use bringing them into *this* world, Kathleen, and not preparing them for the *next* one. Can't you see? That's the most important thing we have to do in life. Get those little ones ready for whatever lies beyond. If I don't do that—I've failed as a father. I've failed as a man. Failed miserably."

Kathleen hadn't realized that he felt so strongly about it.

"Don't you know anything about what one is to do?" he

asked her, and there was pleading in his voice. Donnigan needed some answers.

"No. No," said Kathleen shaking her head. "I don't know anything."

Donnigan stood and moved to where his hat hung on the peg.

"Where are you going?" asked Kathleen quickly. She did hope he wasn't going to do something foolish. She was worried about Donnigan.

"To town—for some answers," he said to her. "I'm going to check out that church."

"But the parson's gone. The church is closed."

"I know. But there has to be someone left in town who went to that church before it closed. Maybe he—or she—can help us."

Kathleen wished to say, "I don't need help. I'm fine," but down deep inside, she knew that it wasn't the truth.

———

It seemed a long time to Kathleen before she heard Black coming. The young pup that Donnigan had gotten for the children made a fuss. He didn't get to bark at visitors to the Harrison farm often, so he made the most of it when he could.

Sean finally managed to quiet him. "That's Pa. He lives here, silly," Kathleen heard the boy say to the small dog.

Kathleen had to wait for more long minutes while Donnigan put the horse away and stopped to chat with the children who were playing in the yard.

Kathleen hoped that Donnigan's search had been fruitful. She was tired of seeing him with the deep concern in his eyes.

But when he entered the kitchen, she saw that his shoulders still drooped.

"No luck?" she asked, and he shook his head slowly.

"You didn't find anyone?"

"Oh, yeah. I found an old couple that used to go there."

"But they didn't have any answers?"

"Well," said Donnigan taking a chair at the table. "They did—and they didn't."

Kathleen puzzled over his answer.

"They told me what went on at the church," he began.

Kathleen waited.

"They sang songs—hymns they called them—songs about God—from a special book. They prayed. At least the parson prayed for them. And then he read from the Bible. That's the real key to it all, the old folks said. Then they listened to the parson talk a sermon."

"A sermon?"

"About how to live and what to do and all that," explained Donnigan.

"But he's not there anymore. The church still isn't planning to bring him back?" asked Kathleen.

"Nope. Not much chance of that."

Donnigan stretched out his long legs as though to work the kinks from his body and from his soul.

"Guess there's not much we can do then," said Kathleen.

"If I only had some way to get us a Bible," declared Donnigan. "I asked around town and nobody knows where to get one."

"You mean—we'd just read it on our own?" asked Kathleen. It seemed a bit presumptuous to her way of thinking.

"That's what the old folks said we could do."

Kathleen thought about it for a few minutes. There didn't seem to be any answer to their problem. She was about to leave her chair and go back to peeling potatoes for supper when she had a sudden thought.

"Wait a minute," she said, reaching out and grabbing Donnigan's arm with both hands. "I think I have a Bible."

Donnigan jerked his head up.

"In my trunk," went on Kathleen. "It was my grandmother's, and she gave it to me before she died."

Then she finished rather lamely, "I didn't know it was something you could read. I thought it was just for writing things in. Like births and deaths. That's the only time I saw Grandmother use it. When she wrote things in it."

Then Kathleen's eyes lit up with sudden understanding. "She *couldn't* have read it," she said. "Some English clergyman gave it to her, and Grandmother couldn't read English. I remember looking at the words she wrote. They looked strange, so I asked my father. He said they were Irish words."

Already they were moving toward the bedroom and the old steamer trunk.

Kathleen rummaged around, digging through discarded garments and worn bedding, and finally she came up with a faded black book.

"It *is* a Bible," said Kathleen joyfully. "It says so right here on the cover. See!"

Donnigan reached for the book. He held it lovingly, worshipfully. "Kathleen. I think we have our answer." His voice was husky with emotion.

————

From then on the reading of the Bible was a part of every day. Donnigan always gathered all of the family around right after breakfast and opened up the book. They began with Genesis. It was a thrill for Donnigan to discover how God had created the earth and all it contained. They discussed it with their little family.

"Did He make everything?" asked the chattery Fiona.

"Yes, He did," said Donnigan. "It says so right here."

"The birds?"

"The sky?"

"Worms?"

"Mama?"

"Washtubs?"

"Whiskers?"

"Snipper?" Snipper was their new dog.

To each of the childish questions, Donnigan offered a firm "Yes."

"Really, Donnigan. I don't think He made washtubs," Kathleen gently rebuked him later.

"Well, He made what washtubs are made of—doesn't that count?" replied Donnigan, unabashed.

Kathleen nodded. "Perhaps," she agreed.

————

The older children enjoyed most of the Genesis stories, though they did not understand them all. But when Donnigan got on into Leviticus and Deuteronomy, he had a hard time holding even Sean's attention. And the young Eamon was next to impossible.

"Are you sure we should be reading that to the children?" Kathleen dared to ask. "Maybe it is meant just for grown-ups."

Donnigan wondered the same thing. He decided to do the reading on his own and then share the easier stories with his family in his own words. It seemed to work much better.

————

"We're supposed to be praying, too," Donnigan said to Kathleen one day as he laid the Bible aside.

Kathleen just nodded.

"Do you know any prayers?" was his next question.

"No," she replied.

"I wonder where we can get some," said Donnigan.

"Maybe the old folks in town would know."

"I already asked them. They said the parson did the prayers—and he took the books with him."

"Then I guess we'll just have to do without prayers," said Kathleen.

Donnigan rubbed his hand over the cover of the Bible, saying only, "I really don't think we've got this all figured out."

Chapter Twenty-one

Family

"I was thinking—if this one is a boy—you might like to name him."

They were sitting by the table at the end of a long, exhausting day having a cup of buttermilk together.

"You run out of names?" asked Donnigan lightly.

"Oh no. We could call him Aiden or Keenan or Devlin or—"

Donnigan held up his hand.

Kathleen smiled and took another sip of the cold buttermilk.

"And if it's a girl," prompted Donnigan.

Kathleen tilted her head to one side teasingly. Her dark eyes were shining, her hair, from which she had loosened the pins, tumbling about her shoulders.

She still looks like a child, thought Donnigan to himself and felt a renewed urge to protect her.

"I might even let you name a girl," responded Kathleen after having given the matter pretended serious consideration.

Donnigan nodded. "I accept that challenge."

The baby was another son. Donnigan named him Timothy.

Eighteen months later a baby girl was added to the family.

"Well—who is she?" asked Kathleen as she pulled the wee one close and kissed her soft cheek.

"I would like to say Kathleen after her mama," responded Donnigan, "but since that might get confusing—she's Rachel Kathleen."

Kathleen smiled. Little Rachel. She pulled the baby close and gave her another kiss.

————————

The years had been kind to the family. Never had they faced serious illness or mishap. Except for the loss of baby Taryn, Kathleen had brought all of her babies safely into the world with no problems. They were healthy and ruggedly hardy from farm life.

Donnigan kept their bodies toughened yet agile with a balance of work and play, and Kathleen kept their minds active and alert as they pored over lesson books.

Each morning Donnigan read from the Bible. The children had learned most of the Bible stories over the years, and Kathleen was often amused to hear their childish discussion about God.

"They talk about Him like He was—was a part of their world," said Kathleen to Donnigan.

"I hope He is," responded Donnigan—but his voice was still filled with doubts.

"I mean—like He is—is as real to them as—as I am."

Donnigan nodded. That was how he wanted it to be—but was he doing it right? Was he giving them what they needed? "Oh, God," he often groaned in times of quiet reflection, "give me wisdom. Show me what to do. It would be a terrible thing to prepare them for only this life."

————————

"Why do we always read the Bible?" It was Eamon, their

difficult one, who posed the question.

Donnigan laid the book carefully back on the table.

"Because," he said with great feeling, "that is the only way that we can get to know God—who He is—and who He wishes us to be—how He wants us to live."

Eamon shrugged, seemingly unconvinced—or else just unconcerned.

"We already know about Him," said the five-year-old boy. He had been told the same stories often enough that he should know them by heart by now.

"Do we?" said his father. "Maybe we do. Let's see. Tell me what you know about God—all of you."

Eamon looked surprised.

It was the outgoing Fiona who responded first. "He made—everything." She swung her hand in a big arc to include as much as she could.

"He made the waters come down," said Brenna softly, "an' all the animals went in the boat."

"He's sorta—magic," said Sean.

"Magic? How?" prompted Donnigan.

"He can do things that no one else can do."

Donnigan nodded.

"He deads people when they're bad," said Eamon.

"Kills people," corrected Kathleen, and then felt shock at her own statement.

"He doesn't kill people," argued Fiona, casting a disgusted look Eamon's way.

"He does too," insisted Eamon. "What about the men the earth ate up? And what about when the flood came?"

"The people were already in the big boat," cut in Fiona quickly.

"Uh-uh. Nope," said Eamon, shaking his head emphatically. "Only Noah and his wife and them others were in the boat."

"There were eight," cut in Sean who always listened well to the Bible stories. "Noah and his wife and three sons and their wives."

But Eamon didn't seem to care much about the particulars.

"Well—all the other people got dead," insisted Eamon.

"That's 'cause God was mad," interposed Brenna softly. The fact didn't seem to trouble her in the least.

"I don't dead people just 'cause I'm mad," said Eamon.

"You're not God," Fiona quickly flung back at him. Her voice was shrill and angry.

"Just a minute," said Donnigan. The little conversation was getting totally out of hand and not at all what he had intended.

"Sit down—all of you. I think we need to discuss this."

The children all sat down, as told, though Eamon looked reluctant to do so and was the last child to finally take his place on the kitchen floor.

Oh, God, Donnigan found his very soul crying out, *help me with this. Please help me.*

He turned back to the ring of children—the wonderful yet frightening responsibility that God had given to him. What were the right words? Did he have the truth to share with them? Or was he still dreadfully lacking?

"God made us," he began. "And He wants us good—like Fiona said. But people didn't stay good. Remember the story about Adam. He did bad. And after that it was very easy for all men—and women—to do bad, too."

Donnigan stopped, took a deep breath and licked his lips.

"Now God didn't stop with just making this world," he went on, hoping that he had his thoughts right. "He also made a beautiful heaven. It has everything in it to make us happy—and nothing in it to make us sad. God made heaven for people. But He also made a hell. He made it bad. In fact, He made it just as bad as it could possibly be so that no one would want to go there. So that people would try *very hard* not to go there."

Donnigan stopped again and looked at the little faces around him.

"I don't want to go there," put in Fiona, shaking her head emphatically.

"But people were still bad," went on Donnigan. "God told them and told them to be good—but they liked being bad, better.

"From time to time, there was a man who wanted to be good. To do what God told him. So when God would find a man like that, He would talk with him, help him, and sometimes God even felt that it was important to get the good man away from the bad people."

Donnigan stopped and looked straight at the squirming young Eamon.

"It is very easy for even good people to be—be followers of bad people. God knew that. So sometimes He took the good people away from the bad place where they lived. Like He did with Abraham when He called him away from Ur. Like He did with Noah and his family when He had them build the boat. He sent the flood of water to save Noah and his family from the evil around them. If Noah had stayed with the bad people, his family might have soon become bad, too.

"But sometimes, God used other ways. There were many good people—and bad people mixed in with them. Well, God knew that if the bad people were allowed to stay there and do the wrong things—then it wouldn't be long until other people would be doing wrong things too.

"So God took the bad people away. Like the big earthquake that swallowed them up. Yes—they were killed. That was the way God could be sure that they wouldn't—wouldn't spread their evil—their bad to others.

"You see—God didn't really kill the bad people because He hated them and was in a temper. Oh, He hated the sinful things they did—the way they lived. But God destroyed them so that they wouldn't destroy others—so that others wouldn't learn to be bad, too."

He looked at the little faces before him. Sean sat listening carefully, seeming to take in every word. Fiona listened with her head tipped to one side, her fingers twisting in the folds of her dress, her toes wiggling impatiently in the worn boots. Brenna sat quietly, one arm cradling her doll. She appeared to be listening, but Donnigan wondered if Brenna, the little dreamer, might silently be humming a little tune to her baby.

Eamon stirred restlessly. His eyes were not on his father's face. He was watching a spider that crawled up the outside of the window. Donnigan prayed inwardly that Eamon might have heard more of his words than he had let on.

Timothy, at three, wiggled and listened by turn, seemingly catching a word here and there that interested him, then turning his attention back to the small hole in the knee of his pants.

Their baby Rachel, sitting on her mother's lap, paid little attention to her father's words, though she was intent on studying his face.

Six children—all different—all in need of heaven, thought Donnigan. *God, help me to get them there.*

Eamon continued to be their "tester." Often they heard the same defense: "You didn't tell me not to."

When he cut all the tops off the early spring carrots to feed the bush rabbits in the woods along the creek, when he cropped baby Rachel's silky curls with Kathleen's sewing scissors, when he threw a hen off the barn roof to see if she could fly, when he left the poor pony out in the pasture blindfolded to test if she could see in the dark. At all of these times, and many more, Eamon would shrug his shoulders with the same answer: "You never told me not to."

How could their minds possibly keep ahead of the young boy's?

Timothy, on the other hand, was cheery and cooperative. He followed along after his older siblings, grinning at their accomplishments, clapping at their exploits, seemingly thinking that everything they did was terribly right and brilliant.

Kathleen rejoiced in the small boy. He was such a delightful change from the rambunctious, ever-pressing Eamon. No challenging, no arguments, no talking back.

But Donnigan watched his small son and felt concern.

Kathleen could not understand his worry. "He's so easygoing and pleasant. All the others dote on him."

"That's just the point," replied Donnigan. "He might get the idea that's what life's about. Pleasing others. Being fussed over. You can't always please others, you know. Sometimes you have to take a stand for what is right. You have to be one person against the crowd. Timothy is too quick to try to please. Too quick to do whatever he is urged to do. No. I'm thinking that boy might take more wisdom to raise than we think."

———

Rachel, dear little dark-curled Rachel, began by being a happy, docile baby, seemingly content to watch the actions of the older children. Kathleen was quite surprised to discover when Rachel reached about eighteen months that her independence took a nasty turn.

"I do it!" she would scream and insist on doing her own thing—her own way. Though usually happy if left on her own, she was stubborn and difficult to discipline.

"Why didn't I stop at five?" Kathleen asked herself more than once. But inwardly she knew that she loved the baby dearly and couldn't imagine life without her.

———

"We really should pray, too," Donnigan told his little family as he closed the Bible one morning.

"What's pray?" asked Fiona.

"Well, it's—it's—" began Donnigan.

"Talking to God," said Kathleen to help him out.

"Then let's," said Brenna simply.

Donnigan felt ashamed. How could he tell his children that he didn't know how to pray? Didn't know the words—the procedure? Didn't have any of the prayer books or hadn't learned any of the prayers? Little did Donnigan realize that what he cried from the deepest recesses of his heart—many times every day—was prayer.

He was about to try to explain when Brenna spoke again. "I'll talk to God," she said simply.

"She does it all the time," explained Fiona to her parents.

"But—" began Donnigan. He did not want his child to do anything sacrilegious.

"God," said Brenna, folding her hands in her lap and looking heavenward, "we read all about you in the Book. Sometimes we understand—and sometimes we don't." She gave her shoulders a slight shrug. "I liked the story about Jesus making the bread grow. And Fiona liked the story about the lions with their mouths tied shut. And Sean—" She stopped and looked at her oldest brother. "What did you like, Sean?" she asked him.

"Making things," Sean said, his voice almost a whisper.

"And Sean likes how you made everything—like the animals. He likes the horses best. And—" Brenna stopped and looked around the circle. "Eamon likes the—the way you dead people." Eamon wiggled, then grinned. It made him feel important to be talked about to God.

"And—Timothy likes—"

"The Three Bears," called Timothy excitedly.

"That's not the Bible," said Fiona with chagrin. Timothy looked surprised at the put-down and lowered his face, his lip coming out.

"Timothy likes the bears you made," Brenna changed it and Timothy lifted his face again, a grin replacing the pout.

Brenna cast one last glance around the room.

"And—Rachel likes— She's still too little," she explained to God, shaking her head.

Then she lifted her hands in front of her, looked around the room once more, shrugged her little shoulders and announced, "And that's all."

The prayer was over.

From then on, Donnigan encouraged his children to pray their own simple and original prayers.

Chapter Twenty-two

Eamon

Donnigan eventually knew the Bible well enough to know where to turn for the stories the children would understand—the stories that he thought they needed to know.

They had covered both the Old and the New Testaments a number of times. But Donnigan found himself flipping back to the New more and more often. The stories about the Son God sent to earth held fascination for him—and interested the children.

Kathleen hardly realized how much she had changed over the years she had spent with her family in studying the Bible. She no longer felt the same bitterness, the same resentment toward God, that she had when she had lost baby Taryn.

But when the letters came from Edmund wondering if "they would be kind enough to share the wealth that America had afforded," Kathleen would rage inwardly, looking at the six children round her table that had to be fed and clothed. But she said nothing, and knew without asking that Donnigan always managed to find some way to send a bit of money from their meager savings.

Deep inside there was still an uneasiness in Kathleen. Why did she have to struggle so? Why did her temper still flare when things irked her? Why wasn't she able to put the past behind her and forgive Madam? She believed the Book that Donnigan read each day. She even tried to live by it. So why didn't God help her with her struggles?

Donnigan, too, had inner battles. He had never been troubled by deep anger. It simply was not his temperament. But there were other things that bothered him. He wondered if his offspring didn't get some of their independence from their father. Donnigan always liked to be in charge—make the decisions for those in his care. Hadn't he nearly smothered Kathleen in the first year of their marriage? Was he doing the same now with his children? No, surely not. It was important for them to have the right training. Donnigan felt strongly about it. It was the most important thing in the world to him. But was he doing it right? Doing all he could? He was sure in his heart that God really existed. Sure that the Bible held the truth. Why then didn't he find peace for his own soul?

————

"I don't understand it," said Sean thoughtfully.

He and his father were excitedly surveying the new colt that had just made his appearance in the far pasture.

"Don't understand what?" asked Donnigan, turning to the boy.

"If—God—creates everything—then why—why—how come animals keep making them? Who really makes them—the mothers or God?"

Donnigan smiled.

"God created all things—in the beginning," Donnigan explained. "But when He did—He designed them special so that each thing—in all His creation—could reproduce itself. That is, could make a baby—of whatever it is. The pigs have pigs—the horses have horses." He didn't need to go on. Sean was a farm boy, he knew about reproduction.

"God still has a very real part in everything that is born. He is the 'giver of life' just like the Bible says, but He allows the parents to bring forth young. That's how He made them. Remember those words God spoke in Genesis, 'Be fruitful and multiply'? That's what they mean."

Sean nodded.

"That's how life continues on," Donnigan went on. "Animals, birds, fish, even plants, are still obeying God's command. Are still reproducing. Why, I'm told that the drive to reproduce is even stronger than the drive to eat," he went on frankly. "But without it—life would cease. The old would die off and there wouldn't be any young—any new life—to take their place."

Sean nodded again, willing to accept whatever his father told him. His eyes had not left the new foal.

"He looks like Black," he said, turning Donnigan's attention back to the new colt.

"Young often look like their fathers. Or mothers," said Donnigan, nodding his head in agreement. "But sometimes they don't. Guess the important thing—and sometimes the scary thing—is that they often act like their father—think like their father."

Again Donnigan felt keenly his responsibility to his children.

A young gelding approached the new colt in curiosity and the mare tossed her head, bared her teeth, and flew at him, turning him aside and driving him away with nipping teeth and flashing hooves.

"Why did she do that?" asked Sean. "She knows him. He's just another horse. He wouldn't hurt the foal."

"Parents can be very protective," said Donnigan. "A new mother will often give her life to save her young."

Sean nodded his agreement. He had seen new mothers protect their babies before.

"Guess she'll take good care of him, huh?" he commented as they prepared to leave.

But Donnigan continued to ponder their conversation even after they had turned their mounts and were on the ride home.

Reproduction? It was a strong drive. Animals risked their lives to fulfill the inborn command of God. And that was just to bring an offspring into the temporary world. How much more important that one reproduce spiritual children—children who could be taken to heaven for that eternal life that the Bible spoke of.

That was *his* job—as a parent—and yes, he would be willing to give his life to see that it was accomplished—that his children not be barred from the heaven God had prepared.

Yet, what he was doing—what he was struggling to accomplish—somehow seemed to be falling short. And Donnigan did not understand why.

———

Of all of the children, Eamon seemed to need the tightest rein. Donnigan often felt at a loss as to how to properly guide the young boy. To discipline after the fact seemed like shutting the barn door after the horse got out. If he could only instill in his son a *desire* to do right. But how? Eamon seemed to thrive on controversy—on bucking authority—on testing his parents. Why? Why? Donnigan asked a dozen times a day. Why so much defiance in a child who was loved?

Eamon was not all bad. In fact, he had many good qualities, and Donnigan and Kathleen continually pointed them out to each other and to the young boy, reminding themselves daily to keep those good points ever before them. But so often the rebellion seemed to struggle with the good.

Another thing that caused Donnigan concern was small Timothy. He followed Eamon everywhere he went, copying the actions of the older child, taking whatever order Eamon cared to give.

If Eamon said, "Here. Throw this rock at that old gobbler," Timothy threw the rock. If Eamon handed him a stick and said, "See if you can hit hard enough to break that window glass," Timothy broke the window glass. When Eamon was disciplined for telling Timothy to do such things, he became more clever. He began to say, "Do you think you can tie the goat up by her tail?" Or "Do you think you could make an *A* on the house with this red paint?" Of course Timothy always thought he could, and Eamon could stoutly declare, "I didn't tell him to do it."

It was a bad combination and one that worried Donnigan and Kathleen.

―――――

"Mama, come quick. Eamon is hurt!"

It was Fiona screaming as she ran into the kitchen. Kathleen dropped the bread dough she was kneading and rushed to follow the young girl, her eyes wide with terror. What had happened?

"He played in the fire," Fiona shouted over her shoulder as they ran.

The fire. Donnigan and a neighbor man were getting set to butcher one of the farm pigs. A tub of boiling water was needed for dipping the carcass so they could scrape away the tough bristles. All the children had been thoroughly warned time and time again to stay away from the fire.

Kathleen found the boy in the garden shed, curled in a ball, trying hard to keep from screaming over his damaged hands.

"Oh, dear God," she said after taking one look. Then she turned to Fiona, "Go get your father. Quick!"

She managed to get Eamon to the house. He had given up on being brave and was crying in pain by the time she laid him on the kitchen table. The palms of his hands were fiery red with smears of black soot across them. Kathleen could already see angry blisters beginning to rise.

"Oh, dear God," she cried again. "Both of them. Both of them."

Donnigan arrived and took over. Kathleen felt sick to her stomach. She moved along the table and tried to calm the boy by speaking to him, pushing back his unruly hair, and running her hand over his flushed, tearstained cheeks.

The other children began to gather, eyes wide, voices one minute filled with excitement, then silenced by the enormity of the injury.

"He's hurt bad," Kathleen heard Brenna whisper.

"He shouldn't have played in the fire," responded the

motherly Fiona as she wiped away her own tears.

Timothy just stared—wide-eyed. Then he started to cry. He backed away from the cluster and ran sobbing to the boys' shared bedroom. Kathleen wanted to go to him, but she felt that she was needed where she was.

They cleaned up the damaged hands as best they could, applied some healing salve generously, and bound them with white strips of a sacrificed pillow case.

"I wish he could see a doctor," said Donnigan.

"But that would take hours," responded Kathleen.

"Let's just do the best we can," said Donnigan, shaking his head. "I hope we can keep the infection out of them. If we see even a hint of it—we'll have to take him to Raeford by stage."

Kathleen nodded. They would need to be most vigilant in watching the boy.

———

The story came out later. Eamon had said to Timothy, "Do you think you could drop this big rock in the hot water?"

Timothy had accepted the rock and taken the dare.

But as Timothy approached the fire and its boiling tub of water, he had stubbed his toe on a piece of firewood left to stoke the flames.

Eamon, who was near his side to watch what the boiling water would do to a stone, saw the younger boy fall forward. He lunged to push him aside, and in so doing lost his own balance, falling with his hands right in the hot coals.

So it was Eamon who took the consequences of his own disobedience. And young Timothy saw firsthand the cost of defying orders.

———

The hands were slow to heal. Donnigan worried. First, that the hands might not heal properly at all. Then, how the disobedient, rebellious boy would accept having his natural independence totally taken from him. He had to be dressed, he had to be fed, he had to be groomed and cared for. He could not so much as take himself to the outside privy.

At first he found it very hard. Fiona hadn't buttered his bread right. Brenna hadn't cut his pancake the right size. His shoe came untied the way Sean had tied it. His bed had wrinkles. People were never there quickly enough when he needed them. He grumbled and complained about almost everything. Donnigan would just say quietly, "If you hadn't damaged your hands, you could be doing things for yourself."

Gradually the boy seemed to settle into his circumstances and accept his temporary handicap as his own responsibility.

"I'll sure be glad when I get these bandages off," he would declare, but he didn't chafe and fuss as before.

Kathleen, who daily changed the bandages and clipped away dead and damaged skin, watching closely for signs of infection, knew that she would be glad also.

———

As Eamon waited for his hands to heal, his attitude changed considerably toward the other members of the family. There seemed to be some special bonding taking place between him and each of his siblings. Sean helped him with his clothes and did his farm chores while Eamon tagged along to supervise. Donnigan always insisted that Eamon at least go through the motions of choring. He didn't want him sitting around sulking and being bored.

Fiona took her nursing duties seriously, mothering the boy and making sure that everything that he needed was done just right. Brenna made little games of what she did. "Open your mouth wide so the bumble bee can come in," or "Shut your eyes tight while I wash the freckles off your nose," she would tell him, and then giggle when he obeyed.

Timothy tried to help his older brother, but almost everything that he attempted didn't turn out quite right. Timothy likely taught Eamon more about patience than any other family member. For Eamon did adore his younger brother, in spite of the fact that he often led the smaller boy into trouble.

"When you get all better—" Timothy would often say, and then follow the words with some elaborate plan. Eamon would look at his damaged hands and his eyes would cloud. "I don't think that's a good idea," Kathleen heard him say on more than one occasion. "We might get hurt."

Kathleen figured that Eamon had experienced quite enough "hurt" for some time to come.

By the time Eamon's hands healed enough to use in some fashion, he seemed to be much quieter of spirit.

"Maybe God has used this terrible accident to bring Eamon a—a miracle," Donnigan dared to say to Kathleen as they prepared for bed one evening.

"Oh, I do hope good will come of it," breathed Kathleen as she slipped her long gown over her head. She moved toward the bed and threw back the covers.

"But it is so hard—so hard to see his hands scarred like this," she said with heaviness.

"Better his hands than his soul," replied Donnigan.

Kathleen nodded her head in agreement.

"Now," she said to her husband, "what are we gonna do with Rachel?"

Chapter Twenty-three

The Discovery

Donnigan was poring over the Scriptures again. It seemed to Kathleen that he spent most of his evenings reading portions, scribbling down notations and cross-checking verses.

"What are you looking for?" she asked him, using her teeth to bite off the thread that had just been sewn on a button.

"You shouldn't do that," Donnigan reminded her as he looked up.

She nodded. She knew she shouldn't do it, but the scissors were across the room in her sewing basket.

"We're missing something," Donnigan went on in reply to her question. "I'm sure it's here. I'm sure. If I can just get it all sorted out."

Kathleen made no reply so Donnigan went on, scanning down his notes as he spoke. "God made man—man sinned—so God brought in the Law. If man sacrificed the animals and tried to obey—God was pleased."

Kathleen nodded in agreement. Donnigan's brow was still furrowed.

"You don't think we should still be making sacrifices, do you?" asked Kathleen, a bit appalled at the thought.

"No—" replied Donnigan tapping his paper with the pencil. "Remember the verse that says, 'Obedience is better than sacrifice.' And Christ didn't ask for sacrifice in the New Testament church."

"So all we need to do is obey?" responded Kathleen, somewhat relieved.

"Yeah—but the problem is—none of us do."

Kathleen wished to argue that statement. "I do," she said quickly. "At least—I try."

"That's the point," said Donnigan. "No matter how hard we try—we still don't quite make it. Here in Romans it says, 'For all have sinned.' And again over here, 'There is none righteous, no, not one.' And the verse that really settles it is this one that says, 'All our righteousnesses are as filthy rags.' "

Donnigan laid down his pencil and looked at her. Kathleen's hands had stilled in her lap. It sounded to her as if there really wasn't much hope.

"But something changed," she reminded him. "All those verses about Jesus—why He came to earth—to die. Remember it said that He was the sacrifice—once—for all."

"That's why we no longer need the lambs and bulls," said Donnigan, nodding.

"Then what's missing?"

"I don't know," replied Donnigan slowly, leaning back in his chair and gazing at the open Book before him. "I don't know what's missing—except peace. Why don't I have peace, Kathleen? Why am I still struggling?"

Kathleen did not reply. She did not have the answer.

Wallis called—just at mealtime. Kathleen should have been used to it—in fact, she was—but it always managed to irk her just a bit when she had to leave the table and get another plate for the neighbor man and crowd the children even closer together.

"Wondering how yer crops are doin'," Wallis explained to Donnigan as though that were the reason for his visit.

Kathleen lowered her eyes quickly to her plate so her irritation wouldn't show.

"Fine—just fine," Donnigan replied. "And yours?"

"Fine—just fine." Wallis reached for the bowl of carrots.

Wallis had never really gotten over Risa's leaving. He didn't seem as angry anymore and he had progressed to the point of weary acceptance. He knew she would never be back, as he had hoped for so many months—so many years.

"God made the crops," piped up Rachel. Then returned to her eating.

"Ya sure got a nice-lookin' bunch of spring calves," Wallis said around a bite of warm biscuit.

Donnigan nodded. They were nice.

"God made the calves," said Rachel.

Wallis frowned and took a big bite of potatoes and gravy. After he had chewed for a few minutes, he lifted his head again.

"Did ya get much outta thet rain shower last night? I figured it sure did come at the right time."

Before Donnigan could answer, Rachel said in a singsongy voice, "God made the rain."

Wallis, dumbfounded, looked at the child. Then he turned back to Donnigan. "What do you do, Donnigan? Spend all yer time religioning yer young?"

"Not *all* my time," replied Donnigan evenly.

The silence hung heavy in the room for several minutes. Even the children seemed to sense it and stopped their usual prattle.

Donnigan was the one to break it. "You don't seem to put much stock in religious training," he said to Wallis.

Wallis continued to chew; then he lifted his eyes and replied dourly, "It's not I'm *all* agin it. My folks were plenty religious. I had more'n my share in my growin' up—but a man can go too far with it, seems to me."

Donnigan would have liked to ask, "And how far is too far?" but his attention had been caught by Wallis's earlier statement.

"You've had your share? What? What were you taught?"

Wallis shifted uneasily. He reached up and scratched his uncombed hair with the blunt end of the fork he held in his hand.

"Well, I—I don't know as I recall all the—the— You know the usual, I guess."

"Like," prompted Donnigan, leaning forward in his eagerness.

Wallis still hesitated.

"Go on—please," said Donnigan.

"Well—you know the stuff. God made everybody and—"

"We know that story," called out Timothy. "It's in the Bible."

"Then Eve et the apple—and she gave some to Adam— and he et a bite and then God sent them from the garden and told 'em never to go back."

All Donnigan's children could have told those stories— likely better than the grizzled man.

"Then—" prompted Donnigan.

"Well, then ya got all those stories 'bout those other fellas, Noah and Joseph and Elijah and sech," went on Wallis.

With a look Donnigan silenced his children, who seemed about to explode with their own knowledge of those Bible characters. He was anxious to hear what the man had to say. Maybe he had the last piece to the puzzle.

"And then ya get to the next part," went on Wallis slowly. "Where Jesus is born."

"Go on," said Donnigan.

Kathleen had stopped eating. She leaned forward almost as eagerly as did Donnigan.

"Well, He went about healin' people and helpin' the poor and trying to teach what was the right way to live an' fergivin' their sins an'—"

"How?" broke in Donnigan. "Forgive sins—how?"

"How?" Wallis sounded caught off guard. He also sounded puzzled. "How?" he repeated. "Guess God Almighty is the only one who knows thet."

Donnigan felt acute disappointment. But he refused to give up. "Did you ever have your sins forgiven?" he pressed the older man.

Wallis blushed under his bearded cheeks.

"Me? Not me," he hastened to answer.

"Did you see anyone else?"

"Well—sure—lots of folks." Wallis sounded a bit put out. One wouldn't have attended his church, with his folks, without seeing a good number of folks praying for forgiveness.

"How?" asked Donnigan.

"Well—ya gotta go up front of the church—or wherever—sometimes it was at one of them there tent meetings, an' kneel down and cry some, at thet—they call it an altar, I remember now—ya gotta go to the altar—an' cry and ask God to fergive ya fer the bad ya done."

Donnigan eased upright in his chair. An altar. They did not have one. Kathleen met his eyes.

"I wonder if there's an altar left behind in that church," she said aloud.

"Oh, I'm sure they is," said Wallis. "Church always has an altar."

Donnigan's memory began to stir. The Bible spoke of an altar. When God gave the people the tabernacle, and later the temple, He spoke of the altar. The altar was where the sacrifices took place.

"Did they—did they make sacrifices at the altar?" he asked hesitantly.

"Sacrifices? Ya mean like slayin' things? Naw. They didn't do nothin' like thet. Preacher said we was to give ourselves—a livin' sacrifice."

"A living sacrifice? What does that mean?" asked Kathleen.

"I don't know. Preacher talk, I guess. I don't know."

"A living sacrifice," said Donnigan. "You know, there's a verse that talks about that. I saw it again just last night. In Acts. No—no. Romans, I think."

Donnigan hurried away to get the Bible. He spent a few minutes turning the pages while the rest of the people around the table sat in perfect silence.

"Here it is in Romans 12:1: 'I beseech you therefore, brethren, by the mercies of God, that ye present your bodies a living sacrifice, holy, acceptable unto God, which is your reasonable service.' "

Donnigan frowned—reread the verse, then shook his head.

"It says 'service,' " said Kathleen. "Do you think—?"

"It must mean something about living to serve God," said Donnigan, still studying the verse.

Then he lifted his eyes again to Wallis.

"Do you understand it?" he asked the man.

Wallis scratched his head again. The whole conversation was making him dreadfully uncomfortable—and it was so close and warm in the room. He reached up to loosen his shirt and run a finger around his collar.

"Well, ya can't serve Him when ya got sin—thet much I was told," went on the man. "I don't think He really wants much to do with ya when—when ya ain't yet made yer confession."

"Confession?" asked Donnigan.

"Sure, confession," said Wallis, looking a trifle upset with their lack of understanding. "Ya gotta confess yer sins— thet's what ya go to the altar fer."

Donnigan knew there were many verses that spoke of confession. He made a mental note to look them up and study them that evening.

"Then ya just—just—I think they say—accept," went on Wallis. "Thet's how ya be born agin."

Jesus had used those words with Nicodemus, Donnigan remembered. Born again. Born of the Spirit, Jesus had gone on to say. Donnigan felt excitement. The pieces were slowly falling into place.

"An' thet's all there is to it," said Wallis, wishing to get himself out of his present situation.

"You were taught that—in your church?" plied Donnigan.

"Yep. Shore was," said Wallis without hesitation.

"But you didn't confess?"

Wallis looked up slowly, then shook his head.

"But—why? I mean—if you had the teaching—if you knew it worked—why—?"

To their surprise the man began to shift nervously on his chair. He looked down at his calloused hands and rubbed them together in agitation. When he at last looked up his eyes were clouded.

"It worked—fer others. I saw thet. But—well—I was young. I wanted to—well—to do things my own way—be my own boss. I figured there was plenty of time fer religion when . . . someday," he replied simply.

He raised his arm to wipe his sweaty forehead on his shirt sleeve.

"Weren't thet it didn't work," he went on to say. "It was me. I got feelin' kinda ornery like. Wanted to sow my oats. My mama—" He stopped again. "I was about ready to think on it agin when—when—Risa—"

He stirred again.

"But it ain't been a smart thing to do," he finished lamely. "I ain't had me much peace."

"But—others? You've seen others with peace?" asked Donnigan softly. He just had to know.

"Ya mean when they went to the altar and confessed? Yeah. I did. I sure did." The old man managed a wobbly smile and brushed again at his forehead.

I've got to find us an altar, thought Donnigan. *For all of us. That's what we need—a place to confess—and accept.*

———

Donnigan made a trip to town. The church door was still bolted shut. In fact, there was a double lock on the door. Donnigan rattled the locks, but knew there was no way to open them without the proper keys.

He walked around to the window, pressed his face against the glass and peered in. He could see nothing that he understood to be an altar. There was only a small stand at the front where one could maybe lay a book, and a little railing that went around it. Donnigan was disappointed. If he knew what an altar looked like, perhaps he could build his own.

Sadly he turned away. Then he thought of the elderly

couple he had visited a number of years before. Maybe they would know about an altar. Maybe they even had the key to the door.

But when he knocked on the door, it was a new face that greeted him. "Oh, ya mean old Joseph Reed?" said the woman. "They moved off to somewhere. We been in the house for 'most a year now. No, I don't know where they went. He was rather poorly. 'Spose they went off to kin somewhere."

Again Donnigan felt disappointment. As a last resort he headed for Lucas.

After a time of small talk and inquiring of Erma and their four girls, Donnigan dived right in.

"You're a man who has lots of knowledge about lots of things. What can you tell me about an altar?"

"An altar?"

Donnigan nodded.

Lucas sat quietly thinking, seeming to be reaching for answers.

"Well, the Incas used them for their—"

"I'm not talking Incas here," said Donnigan. "I'm talking the Lord's altar, the one church folks use."

Lucas was silent for a minute; then he confessed with no seeming shame, "I've never researched religion," and Donnigan was disappointed again.

———

Donnigan went back to the Bible. He studied the altar in the Old Testament that had been built of shittim wood and overlaid with pure gold. Was that really the kind God demanded? If so, it was no wonder it hadn't been left behind in the locked-up church, and if so, there wasn't much chance of Donnigan getting one.

Donnigan shifted instead to the study of confession and acceptance.

He found a lot of verses. He began to put them together. As he studied they began to make a lot of sense. He reread many of the New Testament stories. The preaching of John, the calling of the twelve, the conversion of Paul—then the ministry of the disciples. As he read there seemed to be a new understanding coming to him.

Confession. Rebirth. That was what was really happening. Over and over—the people who were told of Christ and became His followers were being received through confession of their sin and acceptance of His forgiveness. And Donnigan didn't find one verse where it talked about needing an altar in order to be "reborn." He jotted notes quickly as he went from passage to passage. His fingers were trembling and his face pale. Was that it? Was that the answer he had searched so hard to find? The one that should have been so obvious from the beginning?

It was all there. There were no missing pieces. It all fit beautifully together. You bowed before a merciful God, confessed your sins, and begged His pardon. Then you accepted, with thanksgiving, His sacrifice on the cross on your behalf. He was the Lamb. The Lamb killed and offered up for every sinner. He washed away your sin stains with His own blood and made you clean so that you could present yourself as a living servant of God the Father. And you did not need an altar. God accepted you wherever you were. At whatever time you came with your confession.

God had accepted Saul in the middle of the dusty road to Damascus. The Philippian jailer in the dank, dark dungeon. The Ethiopian in the carriage under the hot sun of the desert.

"Kathleen. Kathleen," Donnigan said excitedly. "I've found it. I've found it. It was here all the time. Look—right here. You don't need an altar. There can be peace—real peace for all of us. All you need is here in this verse. Look! 'If we confess our sins, he is faithful and just to forgive us our sins, and to cleanse us from all unrighteousness.' "

Donnigan looked up, his face flushed with excitement. "Now all we need is to find the prayers so that we can pray them," he said.

They were getting closer.

————

Donnigan shared the verse with his family the next morning, the thrill of his new discovery edging his voice.

They looked at him, some eyes uncaring, some showing confusion, and others registering no response at all.

"What does it mean?" asked Fiona candidly. "What's confess?"

"Well, you remember that we talked about Adam sinning—and then every one of us since that time finding it very easy to sin after that?"

Fiona nodded.

"Well—confessing is admitting that you have sinned. Here—here's another verse. It talks about repenting. Repenting is feeling sorry about what you have done wrong and turning away from doing it anymore. So you admit to God that you have done wrong—and you feel sorry about doing it."

"Like Eamon and the fire," put in Timothy. "He told Mama he did it—and he was real sorry."

Donnigan could not help but wonder if young Eamon would have been sorry if he had not burned his hands in the incident.

"God hates sin," Donnigan went on to get the lesson back on track. "Sin spoils everything. He can't allow sinful people to go to His heaven. The sin would spoil heaven, too."

Donnigan intended to continue his explanation, but a quivering voice stopped him. It was the small Brenna who broke in. "Daddy."

Donnigan turned to look at his child and was surprised to see that her eyes were filled with tears and her chin was trembling.

"I want to tell God sorry," she sobbed.

For one long minute Donnigan seemed to hold his breath. He was about to say, "But we don't know the prayer—yet." Then he looked at Kathleen. He noticed that her eyes were misted, but she nodded her head. It seemed quite right to let the young Brenna tell God that she was sorry in her own childish way.

———

A short time later Brenna walked away with all traces of tears gone and a smile lighting her petite face.

"I told God sorry and now He's not cross at me anymore," she informed Fiona.

"But you have to be good now," warned Fiona, "or He'll get cross again."

For one brief minute Brenna frowned and then her face brightened. "Daddy said that Jesus will help me to be good—and if I really do something wrong, then I'll tell God sorry again."

"Well—you can't just *plan* on doing that, you know," said Fiona matter-of-factly. "You have to really, really, really try to be good."

Brenna shrugged her tiny shoulders. "I will," she said with a toss of her head. "I don't want to make God sad again."

That seemed to settle it.

———

Donnigan went to his outside work and the children all went to play or to care for chores. Kathleen was left alone in her kitchen with the events of the morning filling her mind. At the thought of young Brenna, her eyes filled with tears. The child had really seemed to understand what she was doing. She had been so filled with sorrow as she cried out her plea for forgiveness. And she had been so filled with joy when she felt her little prayer had been answered.

Kathleen kept thinking about it as she kneaded the day's batch of bread.

"That's really what I need," she told herself. "Perhaps it would take care of the heaviness of heart I've been feeling. I've been trying so hard to be good since we've been reading the Bible. I've been trying so hard to forgive—Madam—but I can't. I guess it's just like the Book says, our righteousness is as filthy rags, because we never quite are able to do what we try so hard to do."

Tears were running down Kathleen's cheeks at the troubling thoughts. At last she turned from the bread dough, wiped her hands on her apron, and made her way to the bedroom. She knelt down beside her bed and turned her face heavenward. "God," she cried, tears streaming down her cheeks, "I'm like Brenna. I want to tell you I'm sorry. For all the wrong—all the—the sin in my life. Forgive me, Lord. Please forgive me—and make my heart clean like you have promised—through—through the blood of your Son, Jesus."

There were a few moments of silence—followed by a softly whispered, "Thank you, Lord. Thank you."

Kathleen could not have explained the deep feeling of peace that was stealing over her whole being.

Donnigan tossed another fork of hay into the manger for the milk cow. He was still shaken by Brenna's simple prayer. Was that what Jesus had meant when He had spoken of becoming like a little child? Donnigan concluded that it well might be. Her faith had been so simple—so complete—her prayer so earnest from her childish heart—and she had walked away with a smile on her face and a lightness to her step.

"That's what I've been wanting—longing for," Donnigan told himself. "But I've been making the whole thing so difficult. Trying to sort it all out—make sure I was doing everything right. And it is as simple as that. Calling out to God—telling Him we're sorry."

Donnigan shook his head. His cheeks were wet with the wonder of the discovery.

"So what am I waiting for?" he suddenly said to Black. "Now that I know—why don't I just—?"

And Donnigan tossed his fork into the pile of hay and fell on his knees in the bedding straw.

"Oh, God," he began. "I come like Brenna. Thank you that you showed us the Way through a little child. We don't need fancy prayers. Special words. We just need to come to you with honesty—and talk to you, Lord.

"Forgive me, Lord. Forgive me and give me your peace and cleansing. Help me to be the husband—the father—that I need to be. Help me to be a living sacrifice. Acceptable to you for the sake of Jesus—your Son—our Lamb. I love you, Lord. Help me to show it—through my life—through obedience."

Donnigan waited in silence—his head bowed—his hands clasped in front of him.

A strange and gentle calm seemed to move into the crude farm structure and surround him. He couldn't have explained why, but he knew that his prayer had been answered.

Kathleen ran from the little house. "Donnigan. Donnigan." He would be so happy to learn that she had found the Way—the One that they had been searching for.

But before she had crossed the small yard she saw the barn door open and Donnigan was running toward her.

"I found it—I found Him!" he called across the short distance.

She could tell by his glowing face that he had something exciting to share.

"You, too?" she called back as she continued to run to meet him.

"And you?" he responded.

"Yes," she laughed, the joy bubbling up within her. "Yes!"

"Oh, Kathleen," he managed just before he reached her.

With shining eyes and overflowing hearts, they threw their arms around each other and joyfully laughed and cried together. Nearby, several small heads lifted and little eyes watched in curiosity and awe.

Then Fiona said simply, "Guess they're happy 'bout something."

"I think *I* know," replied Brenna, her eyes glowing again.